INTO THE HEART OF DANGER

Easily the length of a castle wall, the dragon lay curled around the carcasses of over two dozen dead animals—sheep, pigs, and cattle. The bones were carelessly scattered about the small valley, many snapped in two by powerful jaws. . . .

There was no thought as Cedric lowered his lance and dug his spurs into Pele's flank again, just hard enough to give the horse some momentum. . . . The old knight kept his eye on the tip of the lance, hoping that his aim would find its mark to the dragon's heart.

With a speed that startled Cedric so badly he almost dropped his weapon, the dragon reared up on its hind legs and spread its great black wings, blotting out the dying rays of the day. . . .

The Elfwood Series from Ace Books

ELFWOOD
TWISTED DRAGON

Elfwood

Twisted Dragon

KEVIN STEIN

ACE BOOKS, NEW YORK

This book is an Ace original edition,
and has never been previously published.

TWISTED DRAGON

An Ace Book / published by arrangement with
Bill Fawcett and Associates

PRINTING HISTORY
Ace edition / April 1993

For information address: The Berkley Publishing Group,
200 Madison Avenue, New York, NY 10016.

ISBN: 0-441-83326-8

Ace Books are published by The Berkley Publishing Group,
200 Madison Avenue, New York, NY 10016.
The name "ACE" and the "A" logo
are trademarks belonging to Charter Communications, Inc.

PRINTED IN THE UNITED STATES OF AMERICA

10 9 8 7 6 5 4 3 2 1

Chapter 1

WHEN THE SUN ROSE IN THE MORNING, CEDRIC FOUND THAT HE often remembered the times when he was a knight-errant in the forested land of Albion. With the disappearance of the dew clinging to the soft tapestries of grass, images wafted to him that were brash and colorful, like the stories his grandsire had told when knighthood had been new and quests bold.

Pushing himself up against the wall near his bed for support, Cedric felt a familiar backache from sleeping in his chain mail. He swung his legs over and put his feet on the cold floor with a groan and the harsh rub of creaking bones, briefly considering returning to his rest. He sat still for a moment, wondering if, in his youth, he'd ever doubted that all in knighthood was excitement and rescuing fair maids.

Cedric's faith had never been shaken, though he had been challenged on many occasions. Now there was a voice in the back of his mind that wouldn't permit him to even consider the idea that knighthood was not the perfect way of life, and that chivalry was a code that would dictate his actions till death. As he arose, swaying slightly under the fresh weight of his armor, he thought that he recognized the voice as that of his long dead, beloved father.

The little chamber was near the west side of the castle, so that in the morning it was very cool, and by evening, uncomfortably hot. Unfortunately, the old knight preferred it the opposite way, as he liked the sun on his face when he rose and found it was easier to sleep when it was cold. Cedric had once considered complaining about these arrangements to the lord of the castle, Penwarden, but decided to simply accept his lot without a grudge. The lord often said during the few occasions when he honored his men with his presence at dinner that he had too many knights under his aegis, and that he could not afford to give them all the housing they desired, but perhaps one day, if there was time enough and money to spare, he would have quarters built within the castle's high walls.

Cedric liked neither that speech nor the way that wine flowed so freely at these dinners that included no prayer before the meal and no services afterward. Rubbing the muscles underneath his mail and walking to the free-standing basin filled with water, he splashed his face and thought unhappily about the number of times the lord of the castle had made that same promise but delivered nothing. Still, Penwarden ruled these lands and his word was law; he must be doing everything in his power to deliver. And if Cedric thought poorly of the meals, he knew that he did not have to attend.

Cupping his hands and drinking from the basin, the old knight frowned. He had not noticed that the water was as warm as the grass in the midday sun. Spitting out the entire mouthful, he toweled himself dry on a tattered rag that was soiled from lack of proper washing and threw the cloth back onto its peg.

Something clattered to the floor behind and Cedric spun and reached for his sword, but grasped only air since he did not sleep with his weapons strapped to his waist. His sleepy eyes had difficulty in adjusting to the gloom, and he guessed that the sound had been a rat, or perhaps some insect, that infested this end of the castle. Annoying as the vermin were, he never broached the subject to his lord. He had lived in worse places before settling in Penwarden.

Directly over where his heart beat, the old scar along his chest itched, and he reached under the clattering links of his mail and remembered the battle where he had received that wound. His opponent had been an evil man wearing fairy armor, black as pitch. Cedric's blood flowed more quickly when he remembered the pain of the wound and the feel and scent of his own blood as it ran down his armor, pooling at the ground. His two-handed return stroke had been valiant and strong, cleaving the black knight like a tree felled in a forest. Cedric rubbed harder on the scar and spat into the basin again; the evil man's cursed armor had done nothing to save him from the might of an honorable knight.

Sighing, Cedric dropped his hand to his side as the cold crept back into his bones. That fight had been many ages ago, and recently there had been much less glory to gain. With a final stretch, he began donning the rest of his armor, his chestplate, greaves, vambraces, and finally the tabard that was the symbol of his family, rich blue trimmed with gold. He ran his hands over the thick fabric and felt the pattern of the three fleurs-de-lis change the run of the cloth. Reaching under his belt, he pulled out the heavy signet ring and kissed its gold before returning it to its place.

The voice of his father came back to him, as did the face of his grandsire, and for a moment he was overcome by a great sadness. They spoke of the line of his family, great knights and lords and men of honor. Cedric knew he was the last of his line and nobody would wear the noble crest again. To him it was a great shame.

The old knight normally left his weapons in the armory, but this morning he had a special mission to undertake and had kept his broadsword, great-sword, and dagger near him. He had prayed on his knees before his bed for many hours before retiring, and had eaten very little. Strapping his smaller blades to his side and taking the two-handed sword in hand, Cedric left his chamber, slamming the door firmly shut. The doorjamb had warped with age, and the door itself was so old that it often left a small carpet of splinters on the floor whenever it was used.

Chain and plate created a music that Cedric had heard many times before. Some of his fondest memories were of great battles when scores of knights would walk the corridors of castles, armor and weapons clashing with martial timbre. This made his step lighter, despite the morning's aches and disappointments.

The keep was not very large, at least not as large as some that Cedric had been through. It did not take him long to make his way to the feasting hall, where two of the younger knights were finishing the dregs of their wine. Cedric did not like the idea of drinking spirits in the morning, but had learned to keep his tongue when the others ridiculed him for his stolid ways; he knew that there was nothing he could say to change them.

Danforth, a thin man with dark hair and well-groomed beard, leaned his chair back and drank lightly from his flagon. He was eyeing the older knight with what seemed like childlike curiosity. Sitting across from Danforth was Huilliam, dressed in scarlet and yellow, his family's heraldic colors. The looks in their eyes and the general disarray of their clothes told the old knight that the two had not yet gone to sleep since last evening's gaiety.

"Good morn to you both," Cedric said, careful to keep his deep voice from booming through the hall. The Voice of Command was a family trait, something to command men and win battles, not bandy with arrogant youth.

Danforth said nothing but raised his mug in salute, bringing it back to his lips for another small sip. Huilliam reached across the table for a plate of fowl, cold, most of its flesh gone from last night's dinner, which Cedric had skipped. With one hand, he tore off a wing and with the other grabbed his own flagon, acting, Cedric thought, as if he had not eaten in days.

"How now, good knight? Where do you today?" Huilliam inquired around mouthfuls of food.

Cedric held back a scowl at the man's seemingly simple words. He felt their barbs well enough, and did not appreciate having an old dialect spoken by his father turned into an insult mocking his age. In silence, he took a pitcher of water and filled an empty cup, drinking deeply. This time, the water was cold.

Refilling the cup, Cedric replied, "Lord Penwarden announced my quest to all last evening I am sure." His voice was strong and even, much deeper than the younger knight's.

Huilliam nodded his head in confirmation, though the expression on his face did not show that he was particularly impressed. Tossing the bone of the bird over his shoulder, he wiped his greasy hand on his leather breeches and drank deeply from his flagon. Cedric waited patiently for the man's reply despite the fact that he desired to begin his mission as quickly as possible.

Staring into the cup of water, the old knight peered at his reflection. His hair was long and scraggly, still dark despite his years though there was a great deal of silver adorning his temples. A beautiful woman had once remarked that his face had been carved of granite and his laughter poured from purest gold, but that had been long ago. The eyes that stared back at him with such force and focus seemed black in the water, lacking the finer colors that either of the younger knights possessed.

Swirling the water in the cup broke the image of the old knight, and he drank until his breath was gone, setting the mug back down on the table. It did not appear that Huilliam was going to speak again, and after a considerable time, Cedric turned to leave.

"Sir Cedric!" Danforth called in a voice that had an almost feminine ring to it. The old knight stopped and turned, keeping his face straight though his anger grew with each moment.

"Yes, Sir Danforth?" he asked evenly.

"Do you really think what the peasants say is true?"

Cedric shrugged slightly, though his armor did not rise or fall with the motion. "That is not important. Lord Penwarden has commanded me to action, and I must go. Do you wish to accompany me?'' Cedric added as a less-than-enthusiastic afterthought.

Danforth nodded much like his companion had and took another sip from his flagon. ''No,'' he replied simply. ''I was merely curious.''

Cedric ground his teeth and turned again, bracing himself for another interruption. With long, impatient strides, he left the dining hall, leaving nothing but the sound of his armor echoing in the chambers and corridors of the castle. He knew that when he was younger he would have instantly leapt at the opportunity to accompany a senior knight to combat a dragon.

The day turned out to be as bleak as the morning had promised. Cedric had gained his favorite charger from the stables, and rebuked the stablehand for not properly brushing or shodding it. It took him less than an hour to re-shoe and groom the great black beast, whose temper had obviously terrified the young hand into lassitude. Cedric had trained the horse himself many years ago, and like him, the charger had often stayed away from others of its kind out of pride.

The early sun attempted to rend its way through the bank of clouds that hung heavy and grey over the land, succeeding once in a while, but remaining mostly obscured. Cedric had been somewhat disappointed that there had been no fanfare upon his leaving the heavily fortified castle, as there had been when he was younger. Being appreciated and adored was one of the greatest joys a knight could know. Glancing at the heraldic pennant hanging from his lancehead, he thought bitterly to himself that he should have expected nothing less from those in the keep.

The charger's hooves threw great clods of dirt into the air with each powerful step. They made a soft cadence on the canter, and the jangle of harness and scrape of full plate armor was a rhythm that Cedric knew well. The woods to his left reminded him of a time when he had once been caught in a dark forest by bandits, and since he could not see, he was forced to listen to the timbre of the hoofbeats and music of the armor to determine the strength of his assailants.

"Hyah, Pele!" Cedric rasped to the horse, the slight smile that had cracked the veneer of his face vanishing quickly.

Cedric was tempted to run the horse as fast as it would go, if for nothing more than to give it some exercise and him some small rush of excitement. He wanted to reach the battle site as quickly as possible and break lance against the scaly hide of the great serpent that rampaged across the land, terrifying the farmers and eating their cattle. Dragons were something that he guessed every knight hoped to engage in combat, a horrible creature from the bowels of the earth, breathing fire and spitting venom. To vanquish so powerful a foe was the most glorious thing in the world, next to being given knightly spurs and title. He smiled again, widely this time, unbridled and happy.

Taking a deep breath, Cedric calmed himself. The talk of peasants was never a thing to believe; they exaggerated everything. He remembered once that a group of peasants imagined their village overrun by witches and demons, when in fact the "floating heads" and "horrible wails" had been nothing more than the pranks of children. He remembered another time when a "devil-sent" bear had been eating the sheep of a farmer; the man had travelled over a week on foot to reach the hall of his lord, who had sent a young Cedric to investigate. The bear was large, but by no means from Hell.

Cedric felt a rush of heat in his face when he recalled the gratitude of the farmer's daughter.

"Just another bear," the old knight sighed, staring back up into the sky and hoping the sun would appear. At least that would make this day more tolerable.

Since the vale was supposed to be no further than a day's journey from Castle Penwarden, Cedric had packed no more than was necessary for such a trip. He soon discovered, however, that the information had been incorrect and he was going to have to spend another day on the road. Now he would have to hunt and forage for his food. He silently cursed the peasants who had given his lord the supposed location of the dragon, and decided that he did not want to stay in a village overnight as his temper would be short and his tongue, perhaps, too sharp.

Taking another long pull from his waterskin, Cedric guessed that the sun would be setting in another few hours and he would have to find an appropriate place to camp for the night. Though his armor did not weigh heavily on his shoulders, as armor seemed to do when worn by the younger knights at Penwarden, he wanted to take it off and scrub himself down in a stream or river. His chest itched and his body was covered with small red welts where the pinching chain mail had not been affixed properly to the leather padding against his skin. He had taken his helmet off early in the day, but that did not prevent his neck from stiffening.

Rubbing Pele's neck with a gauntleted hand, he whispered, "Don't worry, old boy. We'll stop soon enough."

In answer, the great charger tossed its head and nickered, nodding almost as a human would. Cedric laughed; until now, his had been the only voice he had heard all day.

The path led the old knight around the girth of a large forest, which he had heard was named Elfwood. He had also heard, in the company of his liege, that the lord of Elfwood was an ally but an idiot, to which Cedric gave no credence, despite the source of the information. In his journeys, the knight had discovered that a description given by a man in his cups to another man was rarely true or lasted more than a few days. His grandfather had once said that spirits do not make liars, they just make fools. Cedric had met his share of fools in his time.

Pele stopped in midstride and pawed at the dirt, tossing his head in something that Cedric thought a combination of uncertainty and anger. The knight trusted the senses of his steed more than he trusted the words of most men, and searched the gathering gloom for some sign of danger, some threat. He could see nothing, but donned his helmet and quickly tightened the straps on his armor to ensure a better fit.

The charger walked forward a few more steps, then bucked and pawed at the air, whinnying loudly. Cedric was forced to hang on with both hands, expertly getting his steed back under control. He knew that something that could spook his horse, the horse he had personally trained and ridden into battle against insurmountable odds, must be incredibly dangerous. Loosening his broadsword in its sheath, Cedric took up his lance and pricked Pele's flanks with gold spurs.

The first thing that struck the old knight was the smell of sulphur and corruption rising over the ridge, like a bank of fog that would not give up its tenuous life to the purity of the sun. He lowered his faceplate in the hopes that the visor would block out some of the stench, but the scent penetrated his armor and made his skin burn and itch worse than before.

Easily the length of a castle wall, the dragon lay curled around the carcasses of over two dozen dead animals—sheep, pigs, and cattle. The bones were carelessly scattered about the small valley, many snapped in two by powerful jaws. The remaining livestock had been only half-devoured by the beast, leaving heads staring up into the skies. Cedric watched as one of the dragon's great claws dragged half a cow by its tail and dropped it into its mouth as a child would a bunch of grapes by the stem.

There was no thought as Cedric lowered his lance and dug his spurs into Pele's flanks again, just hard enough to give the horse some momentum. The perfectly lathed lance glittered in the orange of the setting sun as the charger's hooves ate into the soft ground. The old knight kept his eye on the tip of the lance, hoping that his aim would find its mark to the dragon's heart.

With a speed that startled Cedric so badly he almost dropped his weapon, the dragon reared up on its hind legs and spread its great black wings, blotting out the dying rays of the day. The old knight saw that its green body was covered in scales so thick and perfectly spaced that it would obviously take a siege weapon to break it's hide. Despite the fear that threatened his charge, he maintained his deadly pace and watched as the beast's jaw opened wide enough to swallow both him and Pele in one bite.

In the span of a heartbeat, the thought of the great tapestry hanging in the halls of Cedric's father appeared in his mind, Saint George slaying a similar beast. At the same time, the lance disintegrated against the plating of the dragon, shattering the image a thousandfold. Pele jumped high and long at Cedric's expert urging as a powerful tail swept out from behind trying to crush the horse's legs. In a single sweep the old knight drew his broadsword from its sheath and cut at the dragon's wings, scoring a slight gash in the leathery skin but doing little injury.

A gout of perfect flame scorched the ground behind horse and master, the force of the jet sending up hailstones of fire rich in the texture of sulphur. Cedric spun Pele around and bolted to the left, toward the forest, avoiding two large fiery stones and a third, smaller one. The dragon roared so loudly that the trees shook as the old knight approached, and the ground trembled as if with its own fear.

Cedric did not need to turn to see that the monster gave chase, and he would have turned and fought had he the weapons. Something hot bit at his back, and he guessed that in his battle fury he did not notice a hot rock dent his armor. He glanced down and saw that Pele was none the worse. He would have been truly saddened if he had to kill the proud charger, his companion on so many adventures.

Breaking the perimeter of the forest, he thought that this retreat was not the way he would have wanted the battle to end. Despite the fact that he had been skeptical about the dragon's existence, he had secretly hoped for one last chance to bring great honor to the name of his family. As Pele jumped over a fallen oak and the monster bellowed its rage behind, Cedric prayed that the beast would not breathe its fire again and destroy the verdant woods.

Chapter 2

JAEME LOOKED OUT OVER THE EXPANSE OF THE CASTLE COURTYARD and attempted to find the best course to reach his objective, a colorful silk shirt hung atop a post stabbed deep into the dirt. There were very few obstacles between him and the shirt: a small wagon, a trough, a few potted plants. What worried him were the three men instructed to stop him at all costs.

His palm, where he gripped his wooden practice sword, was sweaty and itched. It was either that or his nerves; he could not be completely sure. His padded armor was heavy and stank, clinging to his arms and legs with such tenacity that he was often forced to pull at it just to get his limbs to move. The armor had been borrowed from his friend, not quite the same size and a little thinner, who was seated in a nearby row of tiered benches.

"Come on, Jaeme! It's getting cold out here!" Joseph called out, whirling his sling over his head. He seemed irrepressibly happy.

Jaeme glared at his friend, hoping that the young man's shot with a missile weapon was not as sharp as his tongue.

With the back of his left hand, he wiped a rivulet of sweat away from his cropped brown hair. He wondered how he'd ever let himself be talked into a stunt like this. This was a training session used by all the knights, and as the new Lord of Castle Elfwood, Jaeme felt that he had to prove himself the most able-bodied of them all. In fact, the swordmaster, Desmond, had said outright that there would always be someone better at some skill of arms and they would certainly be older and more experienced. Despite that, Jaeme insisted on outbidding Joseph into the test that now awaited.

The new Lord of Elfwood attempted to relax and ignore the continuing stream of jeers from Joseph, but too many thoughts raced through his mind to allow him much rest. His father's murder was the heaviest of all his burdens, especially since Jaeme was now forced to rule the country on his own, the only counsel being that of a few older statesmen and perhaps the occasional visitor from Albion, the island where the king made his home. He forced himself to remember that, at the moment, the only thing that mattered was this challenge.

"Overcome the immediate," his father had once said.

With a gesture that communicated he was almost prepared, Jaeme held aloft the wooden sword, a two-handed weapon with a heavy leather-wound grip. Normally he would be using a small blade and a shield, but this, like the number of men and obstacles, was part of the challenge bidding process.

"How could I let myself be talked into this?" he asked himself in disgust, bending to stretch the leather of his breeches.

"Some time today, Master Jaeme," Desmond called out, the last man in the course. "If all battles took this long to prepare, there would never be time for peace."

Jaeme nodded once and lowered the sword. Out of the corner of his eye, he saw that a young woman had sat down near Joseph. The first thing that caught his attention was her hair—bright red, living flame. He suppressed any further reactions he might have to her beauty, especially her face, and adopted the stance of a relaxed runner. However, he could not help but hear the silvered peal of her laughter over the whirling buzz of his friend's sling.

Jaeme glanced sharply toward the benches and was surprised to find himself keenly jealous, but he quickly beat the emotion back. Laela had been at the castle for about a month, and constantly peered over his shoulder to make sure that everything was running as smoothly as possible. He often found her frustrating, if not impossible. She thought she knew everything about running a castle and the surrounding lands, and all he wanted to tell her was to mind her own business, even when she was correct.

Without a word, Jaeme bolted forward, running straight toward the first plant. An overweight man named Olbrech waited patiently in a loose stance. Olbrech was older than the young lord of the castle and much more experienced. Jaeme's first plan was to rush forward and dodge to the left in the hopes of using a trick move that would normally cut out a man's legs from behind, had the weapons been real, but at the last moment he changed his mind, continuing the charge. As he approached, he watched the expression on Olbrech's face change from that of confidence to confusion to fear as it became obvious the new lord was not going to slow his pace a step. Obviously unsure of what to do, the overweight man shifted his feet and changed the position of his shield to cover a more general area.

Jaeme ran headlong into his first opponent, keeping his sword pointed back in both hands, on the right side. The man attempted to slash downward at Jaeme's head, but the two-handed sword blocked the blow as it came up, the momentum of the stroke arcing the weapon up into Olbrech's throat. Without stopping to see the results of his maneuver, Jaeme pressed on.

The young lord kept careful watch from the corner of his eye at his friend in the gallery of benches, knowing that a hit, even a lucky one, would immediately end this test. The fact that he had been goaded into these ridiculous odds made Jaeme fight even harder, a trait on which his father had often commented. Fortunately, there had been no actual bet made, so nothing was going to be gained or lost except some pride. Another time, another bet, Jaeme had cleaned Joseph's chambers out for a month.

Jaeme smiled at that memory despite his growing fatigue and nervousness as he watched the second man maneuver around the plants and toward the small wagon. He had won a bet, which forced the other young knight to give up his favorite horse for a year. He had relinquished the steed after only a short period, but the satisfaction was enough, almost as satisfying as defeating that bloated oaf Olbrech, he told himself.

Jaeme barely leapt out of the way to avoid the cut of the second assailant's weapon, a wicker bastard sword, as the man came crashing down from atop the shifting wagon. Previously distracted by his own thoughts, Jaeme suddenly remembered that there were two enemies to deal with, the immediate and the missile-armed. He dodged to the right in an exaggerated move that obviously confused the other fighter; the bastard sword cut ineffectually at the air, but Jaeme was hard pressed to recover from his move.

The confusion did not last long. The two were soon locked in a straight fight, the young lord wielding his weapon like an axe and cutting down and hard, the other, a battle-hardened man whose name Jaeme could not recall, switching from one-handed to two-handed grips as was needed. Jaeme was glad that the rules did not allow secondary weapons as he locked hilts and breathed hard into the man's face, smelling the scent of exertion. A simple dagger thrust and he would be dead.

In another attempt to confuse Joseph, Jaeme locked the man's leg with his own and pressed to the right, turning them in a quick half-circle. Overcome by his stronger opponent, Jaeme nearly lost his footing as the man quickly reversed the move, using greater weight and leverage to kick the new lord away. The back of Jaeme's thigh hit the wagon's wheel and he stumbled backward, swinging his sword in a tight, basic defense.

The knight's downstroke snapped the wooden two-handed sword in half, sending a show of splinters and slats into Jaeme's face, but he was quick to recover and booted his opponent in the stomach before the return stroke fell. Realizing that he was now at a severe disadvantage, the young lord did what he hoped was the unexpected and rushed the other man as he had rushed Olbrech.

The assailant was prepared for such a move and sidestepped, forcing Jaeme to hold his broken weapon in his left hand and push himself back on his feet using the wagon as support. His left arm went numb from a jarring blow and he turned and saw that the rough edge of the blade had stabbed the man in the shoulder near the armpit, where there was little armor. As he fell, the third opponent became visible just behind him. It was Desmond, his instructor.

For an instant, the young lord entertained the notion of ending the battle. He had unintentionally hurt this man, and wanted to ensure that proper care was taken. However, he realized that Desmond would never forgive such a breach in the rules of the test, and would punish him in some unthinkably taxing manner. Jaeme tore the bastard sword from the man's hand, switched grips, and spun with vicious upswing.

Desmond yelled in pain as his sword was swatted from his hand. Before the trainer could recover, Jaeme beat at him mercilessly until he was satisfied that the man had surrendered, a blow to the chest and another to the abdomen. The young lord cut across the intervening terrain, reaching out for his prize.

A hard rock struck him in the back of the neck, where the leather padding was especially thick. The pain was not great, but Joseph's joyous holler was cold agony down Jaeme's back. That was followed by both the realization that Laela laughed as well and that there were at least a score of stones strewn about the prize-post, against which his friend had obviously been practicing since the test began.

''Excellently done, but I don't think I need to tell you the lesson,'' Desmond said, raising his voice over the victorious shouts of the other knight.

''No, sir,'' Jaeme replied, leaning against the post and

staring up at the brightly colored shirt. The pattern of the cloth seemed to mock him somehow.

Desmond snatched the shirt down from the post and handed it to the new lord of the castle. ''Go wash up and put this on. Your punishment is that you must wear this shirt for a week.''

''But I have—''

''I don't want to hear it,'' Desmond interjected, rubbing his jaw, rough with a few days' growth of beard. Without another word, he stalked away, batting Olbrech on the side of the head and spitting a few disciplinary words.

Jaeme knew that no matter how important the state function, he would have to follow his trainer's instructions. It was his punishment and he would have to learn from his mistakes. Sighing heavily, he looked at the shirt again. He was disgusted with himself.

''I think you'll look splendid,'' Laela said, suppressing a laugh.

Joseph rolled his eyes. ''That's not quite the word I would use.'' He, unlike the young woman, could not keep himself from laughing.

The new Lord of Elfwood looked into the druidess's face and felt more ashamed than before. Ridicule from his friends he could deal with, but the same treatment from a woman, especially one who constantly tried to get the upper hand in all matters—that was too much. He was about to say something, when the castle guard shouted a greeting and the gates opened wide.

A huge black horse trotted in, giving a whinny so distinctly proud that Laela caught her breath, sure she would never forget the noble sound. A knight in dented armor hung from the mount's back. The chain mail looked blackened and scored to Jaeme as if the man had run through an inferno. With a gesture, he instructed several yeomen to help the knight off his mount and to get the animal proper care and feeding. He ran to the man without waiting for his friends, keeping out of the way of the castle guards.

''What is his name?'' he asked one of the men as the knight was helped away.

''I think he said Cedric, m'lord.''

* * *

''You must believe me, my lord,'' Cedric implored in a strong, commanding voice. He was ravenous, but the food spread out before him was untouched.

The dining hall of Castle Elfwood was empty except for Jaeme, Laela, Dec, who delicately picked at a chicken wing, and the old knight. Laela could not help but watch Dec nibble at his food. To her, his manners were so excruciatingly polite that she wanted to tear the food from his hand and feed it to him herself.

''In truth, I do not doubt your word, Sir Cedric, but we in Elfwood have heard nothing of this serpent,'' Jaeme replied, taking a sip of water from a flagon. He wished that Polonius were still in the castle to aid in this discussion, but the old advisor had left for urgent business in Albion. A few drops of his drink dribbled down the side of the cup and onto the shirt of punishment; he hoped the water would make it dissolve.

Dec coughed lightly into his hand, obviously desiring some attention. Though the three hadn't been together particularly long, both the new lord and the druidess knew that the mage could be the pinnacle of society when it suited him best. Everyone turned to face the magician as he said, ''Actually, there have been no rumors of dragons for hundreds of years.''

''Not since the walls were built by Offa Sarcassm,'' Laela added with a nod.

Cedric knew that he was having a difficult time convincing his hosts of the danger, and the young lord of the castle was just that: young. Too young to have gained any wisdom worth note. Though he appreciated the respect he was receiving, which was greater than he received in his own castle and home, the brightly colored shirt the man wore was inappropriate attire to receive company.

And magicians were typically untrustworthy. Cedric did not know the reason for the new Lord of Elfwood's choices in counselors, but he did not think them wise. Of course, the druidess was a woman, and in that she deserved proper respect until he was convinced otherwise.

"With all respect to the *mage*, 'rumors,' as you call them, must start somewhere," Cedric said, suppressing his anger. "And I have a dent in my armor as evidence."

Dec pretended to cough as he muttered, "Yeah, in the back."

Jaeme quickly poured Cedric a mug of ale and handed it to the old knight in an attempt to dissipate the man's too-obvious ire. "Regardless of the existence of rumor or truth, at the moment there is simply nothing I can do," he said, practically forcing the mug into his guest's hands. He shot Dec a look that could have killed like an arrow, but he knew that the young mage was so used to these silent confrontations in the sorcerer's college that no insult or threat could influence him.

Laela, however, leaned over the table to grab a piece of fruit off a heavy iron plate, planting her foot squarely into Dec's shin to maintain her balance. The magician yelped in pain and surprise, dropping his greasy food into his lap.

"Sorry," the druidess offered blandly with a toss of her shining hair.

Cedric drank deeply from his mug, but the silent battle between the three youngsters did not go unnoticed. Actually, he discovered that the unvoiced conflict informed him he could afford to give more trust to the magic-wielders. They squabbled amongst themselves as compatriots and not as politicians. Still, he wished he could sway them further, especially since he didn't think they were skeptical, merely unsure of the exact course of action. If that was the case, he would provide them with one.

"What is the reason you cannot mount an expedition, my lord?" he asked, letting a hint of interest slide into his voice. He hoped to bait Jaeme into revealing some doubt of the dragon's existence.

Jaeme leaned over and refilled his guest's mug and replied, "We are expecting supplies for the winter from overseas."

Laela toyed with the apple she had plucked from the iron plate. She found herself staring at the old knight, thinking that he must be the most noble man she had ever had the pleasure of meeting. She hoped that the knight might be able to teach Jaeme a few things about running the castle and protecting Elfwood.

"We must also prepare for the upcoming harvest holiday," the druidess added, breaking herself from the spell.

In his single-minded haste to engage the dragon, Cedric had forgotten about All Hallows' Eve. The castles in the area gathered together the farmers' surplus harvests, for storage in preparation for winter. Though the cold seasons were never particularly harsh, there were times when the people needed additional food or wood to survive. Castle Elfwood was known throughout the counties for its fair treatment of its people when it was under the rule of the now-deceased Richard Mortimer; it would probably take every able-bodied man to perform the task. It was obvious to the old knight that Jaeme, Mortimer's son, had every intention of keeping this tradition alive. He found it influenced him greatly.

"I have forgotten, lady," he said to Laela, who was staring at him. For a moment he recalled another woman with fiery red hair much like this girl, but the moment passed and she remained the only vision.

Dec was still rubbing his shin with an expression of pain when he said, "Why doesn't the Lord of Castle Penwarden help you?" His voice had lost all its previous pretension.

"I *am* the help from Penwarden," Cedric answered, taking a small drink from his frothy mug. The foam caught in his mustache, and he wiped it away with the back of his hand.

"When will you return?" Jaeme inquired. Though he was enjoying the company of this stalwart man, he had other responsibilities that needed to be looked to almost immediately. He hoped he could convince Cedric to stay longer. There was something about the old knight that reminded Jaeme of his father.

Finishing another swallow of his drink, Cedric returned, "As soon as I can raise a unit. I have some monies at my disposal." Though he did not want to admit it, he knew that

Lord Penwarden would not provide additional men or equipment to deal with the monster, despite the threat it posed to life everywhere in the county. However, he might be able to hire mercenaries from Albion or one of the kingdoms that were not too great a distance away.

Jaeme stood and ran his hand purposefully over the brightly colored shirt, feeling his face twist in a grimace he could not conceal. Quickly pulling himself together, he said, "You may remain here as long as you wish."

Cedric rose as well, giving a respectful half-bow to the young Lord of Castle Elfwood. Right hand over his heart, he replied, "I thank you, my lord. I accept your kind offer."

Jaeme smiled a wide, genuine smile, which he hoped was not too out of character for the ruler of a castle and the surrounding lands. "Excellent," he said. "Now if you will please excuse me, I have important business to attend to. I hope to see you at dinner tonight."

Cedric bowed again. "No doubt, my good lord."

Jaeme could not suppress his smile. He bowed in turn, bowing also to Laela but giving Dec a stern glance of disapproval. As usual, the young mage was seemingly unaffected. The new Lord of Elfwood turned on his heel and strode out from the hall, planning the rest of his busy day. Somehow, he had to muster as many men and wagons as possible to retrieve the supplies from the coast without disrupting the operation of the castle.

Laela found that she was staring at the old knight again, and forced herself to turn away. There was something about the man that reminded her of someone else, and from the way he glanced at her, apparently he felt the same way. Though she wanted to talk with him at length, her first mission was to the Druidic Council and their edicts, which meant that she must make sure Jaeme maintained his vigil over Elfwood and ensured its protection.

"If you will excuse me, Sir Cedric," she husked, standing and pulling her long skirts out from under the chair. The green clothes she wore were the color of leaves, and both Dec and Cedric noticed the way they complemented her eyes. Feeling the men's gazes upon her, Laela left the hall as quickly as possible without being too obvious about it. She didn't have that much experience with men, and she knew that there were many things for her to learn, such as how to cope with stares. Jaeme had been staring at her more often of late. . . .

Dec swung his legs out and propped them up on the table, folding his hands over his chest and peering at the old knight through crafty, slitted eyes. Cedric sat back down and regarded the young mage with an equally calculating eye. To him, it seemed that the sorcerer was about to attempt some repartee, doubtlessly for some personal goal. The old knight did not doubt that the magician's skill at banter would be as practiced as his sharp tongue.

However, Dec sat up straight, placing his feet firmly on the floor. He allowed his expression to become soft and amiable, and found that he was actually filled with wonder. This tack confused Cedric, but he was ready for anything.

"Can you show me the dragon?" Dec asked politely, his eyes widening with hope.

Cedric was not prepared for this. For a moment, he could say nothing, but then he stammered, "I must gather a war party together first."

"But if you show me the dragon, I may be able to help."

"How?" Cedric asked, suspicious again of mages and their art.

Dec shrugged. "I don't know. Maybe if I can give a good description to my instructors on Albion, they can assist us."

That was a course Cedric had never thought of. He considered the ruler of Albion a just and noble man, and if the king trusted the magicians of Albion, then he, Cedric, could as well.

"Very well, Decutonius Consulus. I will take you to see the dragon first. Assuming it is still there," he added.

Dec stood up so quickly he knocked his heavy chair over backward. He immediately rummaged through the pockets of his loose robes and pulled out numerous bags full of ingredients for sorcery.

‘‘Great! We’ll leave tomorrow!’’ he exclaimed, his excitement a halo on his face. ‘‘But there’s one more thing.’’

‘‘What?’’

‘‘Call me Dec.’’

Chapter 3

JAEME'S THOUGHTS WERE ON MANY THINGS THE NEXT MORNING. He had attended to at least three minor questions of state after meeting with the old knight, but his mind had been elsewhere. He felt that he could implicitly trust Cedric, despite the fact that the knight hailed from the castle of Lord Penwarden, rumored to be among the landholders plotting against Elfwood. However, the story of a dragon seemed a little far-fetched.

Peering up from his washbasin, the new lord of the castle looked deeply into his own brown eyes and found a great deal of confusion. The water ran down his face and seemed like sweat. He also saw someone unsure of his own abilities to command any number of people and properties, let alone himself. He was a good fighter, though not a very good knight. He wanted to earn the title fully as any other noble, rather than buying into it, as he knew some of the knights in Penwarden had done.

Jaeme stared deeper into his eyes, into himself, at the second thought of Penwarden. That name was cropping up a disturbing number of times this morning, and he would have to keep a close watch for any reports concerning that seemingly polite lord.

The punishment shirt hung like a garish flag to Jaeme's failure on the chair near his bed. He had stared at it all night, his moods shifting with each hour. At first he had felt angry at himself for failing and becoming too enthusiastic about his apparent victories, which he now attributed more to fortune than to skill. Then he was saddened, mostly because the test meant that he was not ready to become a better knight as quickly as he hoped.

By the end of that evening, though, when the sun threatened to break the night sky, he had laughed out loud, thinking of the expression on his own face in contrast with Joseph's. Joseph had not laughed at him, but at victory for his side. Jaeme corrected himself; perhaps his friend had laughed at him to some degree. After all, the test had been silly in the first place.

What hurt most was Laela's comment, or rather, that she had appeared at the lesson in the first place and spoken of the failure afterward. Jaeme was not used to having a woman so close to him all the time, and his experience was lacking in many areas of society where women were involved. Toweling his face dry, he attempted to recall any experiences that had been particularly interesting with a girl, but nothing sprang to mind. Folding the cloth neatly and hanging it on a small rack to dry, he realized that this was just another in a long series of lessons he would have to learn, and learn from people like Desmond and Sir Cedric.

Jaeme peered out the window over the expanse of the castle and some of the surrounding lands. The sun was low in the east, and this was one of the many times that he wished his father were here to guide him. He would be riding to the coast in an hour to get the winter supplies from the incoming ships, and he wanted to be sure that he received enough, and at fair prices. These were matters that his father had offered to explain at some point or another, but Jaeme had found himself too busy with other things, riding, hunting, learning the sword and lance. Now he could not understand how he thought any of those activities could be more important than what the dead king had said he would explain.

"Enough!" the new Lord of Elfwood said to his reflection, finally turning away. He saw that his earlier confusion was gone and that his jaw was set into a firm line, as his father's had been when there were important decisions to be made. This alone gave Jaeme confidence in himself, and he donned the shirt of punishment as if it were a testament to his newfound faith.

"Nobody has seen either of them?" Jaeme inquired, eating the last of his breakfast standing.

Laela shook her head, the bright halo of her hair cascading into her face. "No. They left before the dawn," she replied, brushing the hair away with a hand.

The air this morning was cold, and Jaeme drank down the last of his hot cider, shivering slightly. His breath rose out of his nose and mouth in long, pale plumes, and the fog this morning was unusually heavy and apparently had no intention of going away. The new lord was disturbed by the news, both because Dec was being irresponsible again, not telling anybody where he was going, and because Cedric had left before Jaeme could ask for assistance. He had decided to inquire if the old knight would be willing to lend his experience in the matter of trading with the ships and controlling the men who would unload the supplies. Though this was not normally the lot of knights, Jaeme felt that Cedric had done more than his share of work in the name of safe trade and commerce.

Looking carefully at his companion, Jaeme saw that Laela was shivering uncontrollably though she wore a heavy cape and equally heavy clothing. He motioned for a servant to bring in another mug of hot cider, for which the druidess thanked him with a smile.

"I fear I may never be free of this chill," the young woman muttered into her drink, taking a deep sip though the brew was obviously hot. "This is the fifth mug I've had this hour."

"Perhaps you should stay at the castle, then," Jaeme offered in concern. "I'm sure that my advisors and I can—"

Laela waved her hand in negation. "No, no, I'll be fine. It is my charge to assist."

The new Lord of Elfwood did not need to be reminded of

the druidess's charge. There had been many times since they first met that he desired her to be long gone from the keep. However, most of the time he was glad for her company; there were very few people his age with whom he could talk, at least people who could be with him for the majority of the day.

Jaeme looked at Laela again and thought of her beauty, and then her power. The woman had the ability to transform herself into animals, which was spectacular unto itself, but he found himself attracted to her in ways that he had never before felt for another. An accidentally dropped pitcher of water broke him from his reverie, leaving only a ghost of the thoughts he had harbored.

Three advisors entered the hall, all dressed in heavy cloaks similar to Laela's. Leker and Teves had family ties to the ancestry of Elfwood, and the third, Sejanus Alavay, was a friend of Jaeme's father. They had helped bring the ships from the island of Albion to deliver the necessary supplies, and Sejanus' family owned two of the five vessels.

"When shall we leave?" Leker asked, stroking his thin red beard. Teves stood behind him and shuffled back and forth from foot to foot, muttering about the strange cold and impenetrable fog that had mysteriously appeared.

Jaeme glanced about the hall and saw that his party was ready to depart. "If there are no further preparations to be made, let us go now."

Jaeme desired some kind of small action to get his blood flowing, growing restless with the journey. The coast was not particularly distant, but the number of people in the caravan made travel slow. Despite the fact that the unseasonably early cold had let up enough for everyone to remove their heaviest outerwear, the fog remained, choking the ground, shrouding gullies and holes in the trail.

Laela continued to shiver, and Jaeme considered ordering her back to the castle, or at least making her wait until a proper fire could be built so she could be given some warm tea. However, he knew that she would feel this an affront both to herself and her ability as a counselor. He had given her his own fur-lined cloak over an hour ago, for which she had given him wordless thanks.

"Please do not worry for me, Jaeme," the druidess said now, forcing the words through chattering teeth. She drew his cloak more tightly around her. "I'll be fine."

"You said that hours ago," the young lord replied with a sidelong gaze. "Are you sure you aren't coming down with something?"

Laela shivered more violently, then seemed to calm herself through extreme force of will. She nodded once, but did not voice a reply.

He smiled and said mockingly, "I could order you back to the castle."

"Yes, you could, but you know I would follow."

The reply held almost as much cold as the morning had brought, and Jaeme, who had hoped to add a little levity to the situation, turned away with shame. He looked down at the brightly colored shirt of punishment and thought that dealing with this woman was just another of the lessons that he would need to learn.

Everyone in the caravan peered forward at the shout of one of the advance riders Jaeme had sent to scout the coast. Within a few moments, Joseph rode up on the horse that Jaeme had won in their previous bet.

"What did you find, Joseph?" Laela asked in jerking breaths.

The young knight looked closely at the druidess, then drew back when he realized he was being impolite. "Nothing, my lady. The coast is clear, except for the fog."

"I thought the ships would be there already," Jaeme said rhetorically, glancing questioningly at his two friends.

Joseph shrugged. "There is no one there."

Jaeme nodded in silent understanding. He guessed that the ships might have run into some trouble with the weather, or maybe the caravan was a little early. There was even a chance that Joseph's circuit had simply not come across the vessels. "Please tell the counselors, Joseph."

As his friend rode off, Jaeme tried to figure out where the ships might be, and decided that there was no chance Joseph could have missed all five. He hoped Laela might have an idea of the vessels' location, but seeing her body racked by another fit of violent chills, he kept his silence.

The ships were nowhere to be found on the coast, forcing the party to wait past sunset. Jaeme had sent more scouts to search for the vessels, but something in the cold and the fog made him doubt that they would be found.

Standing at the edge of the great rock cliff that created the sheer coast of the land in this particular area, the young lord stared out over the sea and saw nothing but white shrouding mists that did not want to give up their shadowy life to the dying light of the sun. He had never seen anything like it, and behind him heard some of the men whispering that they, too, did not know its like.

Sighing with heavy thoughts, Jaeme made his way back through the darkening bivouac, skirting around small fires whose heat only extended to the face of the men staring into their depths and no further. The fog had the effect of dampening even that.

"This ain't natural," a battle-hardened man said to himself, mumbling and attempting to rub some life back into his numb fingers. The man's companion, slightly older but no less wise, nodded agreement. Jaeme saw that their eyes were blank and glossed over, as if their lives were being drained by spectres in the mists.

There were a hundred people in the camp and not one of them spoke above a whisper. Had this been a time of war, the new lord of Elfwood would have assumed that these men and women were in rout after being defeated at the hands of an enemy. Nobody here had expected the fog or the cold, and certainly none expected the ships to be missing. Jaeme had asked his counselors what could be done about morale, but Leker and Teves were doing everything they could to keep themselves warm and offered no advice. Alavay was off searching for his ships.

Pushing the heavy flap back from his wagon's entrance, Jaeme saw that Laela was lying on the floor curled up into a ball, hugging her knees tightly to her chest. It seemed to him that she was sleeping, though chills continued to rack her thin frame. Releasing the flap, the young lord walked to a nearby fire and removed the teapot suspended there on a tripod, using his cloak as a potholder. Grabbing a metal cup from one of the pegs on the outside of the wagon, he stepped back inside and poured the druidess some of the pungent brew.

Actually, Jaeme was unsure if he should wake her and was about to leave when she rolled over and stared him directly in the eye. For a moment he was startled and spilled some of the hot tea on his leg.

"Damn!" he cried out, brushing at the spill.

Laela's laugh was cut short by a strong cough. Jaeme crouched down and handed her the cup, urging her wordlessly to drink.

"It does sound as if you are sick."

"I don't understand," the young woman replied between careful sips. She breathed in the aroma of the drink, which reminded the young lord of the forest and hot summer days. "Yesterday I felt fine. Now I can't stop shivering."

Jaeme leaned back against a wooden bench, watching Laela gather more blankets about herself. "What do you think it is?" he inquired.

"I've never felt this way before. It's as if I'm sick inside. Not just in my body."

"I don't understand."

"You know," the druidess said with an ambiguous gesture. "Inside. In the soul."

Jaeme was not sure what she meant in the slightest, and could only return a puzzled gaze. He thought about humoring her, hoping that she would not see through his thin disguise, but he knew that she was an able enough reader of his face and emotions to know when he wasn't being sincere. It interested and frightened him.

Laela sighed heavily and gave up. She could tell that her description was not accurate enough, or rather, concrete enough, for someone like Jaeme to understand. Someone who had never felt the ground beneath the padded feet of a cat or the wind rush through the feathers of a hawk. For her, the soul was not merely a part of her life, but of the life of the world as well, the life of Elfwood.

"What is it like to be an animal?" the new Lord of Elfwood inquired, curious at his own insight. For some reason, he thought this is what the druidess was thinking about.

Laela was almost too stunned to answer. Jaeme's question was so astute that she felt a thrill run through her body, a feeling she did not quite understand but which spoke of something related to her as a woman. Within a moment she was shivering again and could do little but drink once more from the near-empty mug.

Jaeme took the teapot, reheated it over the fire outside, then returned to the wagon and refilled Laela's cup. Then he wrapped the still-hot teapot in one of Laela's blankets and tucked it in close to her body. When he was finished, he sat down again, a comfortable distance across from her.

Laela was touched by the gesture, and flattered that the young lord was so attentive; but she didn't forget that the man resented her presence in many ways. Gradually, the penetrating warmth of the teapot brought her some measure of relief.

"I guess being an animal is like the difference between being a squire and being a knight," she finally answered.

"How's that?"

Her reply took a few moments to formulate. "A knight is better than a squire in many ways, but can never leave the essence of the squire behind."

Jaeme fixed her with a questioning look as he considered the answer, but could not fully relate it to the transformation into an animal. He wondered if she meant that it was better to be an animal than a person. He blinked his eyes in confusion and decided not to press the matter further since the druidess was not feeling well.

Gazing down at Laela's red hair and fine features, Jaeme suddenly had the urge to burrow his way under the blankets with his guest, in the hopes of relieving some of her discomfort by adding his body heat to hers. However, he quickly checked himself and wordlessly questioned his motives.

The young lord half-rose and walked to the entrance flap, deciding that honor and valor would rule the day. Turning back, he asked, "Is there anything else I can get you?"

Laela shook her head and closed her eyes. "No. Nothing thank you."

Chapter 4

"HAIL, HAIL!"

"Who goes there?"

"Orange."

"Orange who?"

"Orange you glad I won't tell another of these jokes?"

Dec burst into a peal of laughter, slapping his knee in exaggerated mirth. He had spent most of the morning attempting to speak with the old knight, but had been unable to elicit even the most minor response. In many ways he was disappointed. He really did respect the man, secretly respecting anyone of great age and merit. He thought wistfully about Old Squintum at the magician's college on Albion who had been the butt of so many of the young sorcerer's pranks. As it was now with Sir Cedric, Dec had never meant any disrespect; he knew he only wanted to make things a little less grave.

With a secret sigh, he asked, "How many knights does it take to fix a wagon wheel?"

Cedric ground his teeth, but in the spirit of honoring the

new Lord of castle Elfwood, he weathered the magician's verbal baiting without complaint. "How many?"

"Two," Dec replied, holding up his fingers. "One to break out the wine and the other to curse the peasants!"

The old knight withstood another round of exaggerated laughter. He tried to ignore the young man's incessant prattling, but found that he could not help himself. When he had first met the mage, Cedric expected to find someone cold and crafty, manipulating Jaeme toward an unknown agenda. Now, after riding with the lad for the better part of a day, he found little except youthful impertinence and perhaps a genuine need for attention and respect.

Glancing back, Cedric saw that Dec was not as heartened by his own voice as he pretended. The cold and the fog were wearing on the boy's spirit. With a heavy sigh, Cedric turned back and attempted to find some line of conversation to bolster their morale, his as well as Dec's.

"One of my ancestors fought a dragon," he began slowly. "He was no older than you."

Dec was startled by the turn in conversation and eager to learn more about Cedric. However, he did not want to seem *too* enthusiastic, as that might imply he was not as calm and carefree as he wished to appear. "Truly?"

The reply was more of a statement than a question, and to Cedric that meant the boy was not interested in anything but annoying ramblings. However, the ancestor in question deserved at least the honor and respect of having his name mentioned.

"Yes. Sir Morgan of Ancalagon, from the land that is now called Albion."

There was a short time of silence, broken by the dull thud of horse's hooves muffled in the fog that maintained its sickly vigil over the earth. Dec's mind was far away. He was thinking of his home on the main island and wondering how his mother and father were faring. And, for some reason, a picture of the sun appeared in his thoughts from the last scroll he had read before leaving. He had borrowed the parchment from the library at the Magisterium Lundinium without asking and studied the beautiful illumination and associated cantrip. He did not understand why this image should appear and banished it with a shrug.

Cedric glanced inquiringly at the boy, but decided to let the mage have his privacy. Instead, he said, "Sir Morgan was one of the bravest knights in my family. He was loved by all."

"All who?"

"What?"

"Loved by all who? Who loved him?" Dec asked innocently.

"Why, everyone he met," Cedric replied, turning with confusion and anger. "The people in his keep, the peasants that tilled his lands, his wife and family, the—"

Dec turned away and whispered under his breath, "Doesn't sound like much of a knight to me."

"What?" Cedric bellowed, spinning Pele around in a tight circle, stopping the march. His hand went reflexively to his broadsword, but he checked his motion. "What do you mean by that?"

Dec's eyes opened wide with fear and he reined his mount so hard it backpedaled. He stammered a few words, then finally spit out, "I thought knights were supposed to be feared and respected."

The answer shocked Cedric almost speechless. "How many knights have you known?" he inquired slyly.

"Few," the young mage replied with a shrug, keeping his distance. He was not sure why he had made the comment that started this conflict, but wished that he had never said it. Dec had never intended any insult toward his travelling companion who had graciously allowed him to join the hunt for the dragon.

The old knight breathed out a deep sigh and dropped his hand. With a half smile, he whispered, "A knight must also practice temperance." Pele turned about and they began walking again; Dec was confused, and afraid that his ignorance of knighthood had cost him a possible friend.

"Please excuse me, Master Mage," Cedric continued. "I would have thought that someone of your obvious status would have more—experience, with men-at-arms."

Dec's reply was meek: "My time was always spent in study." He knew that this was too true, and thinking back to the college made him wonder how he ever endured.

"Then let me tell you that a truly noble knight is one who is loved by his friends and respected by his enemies. Chivalry demands that might never be used in the name of evil."

"How—?" Dec began, unsure if he should ask the question. After a moment, his curiosity got the better of him and he continued. "How do you know evil?"

Without turning, Cedric pursed his lips and nodded to himself; Dec's question was one he had considered often. "You will know evil when you see it."

"Such as the dragon?"

"Yes. Such as the dragon."

The two travelled for several more hours. Cedric noticed that the journey should not be taking so long, for the plain where the dragon had slept was no more than a long day's ride away.

Orange rays from the sun were diffused and appeared strangely menacing through the mists that permeated the woods. The fog clung to the horses' legs and its cold found its way into the crevasses of the old knight's plate armor. The chain mail was chilly against his body, and he suppressed a shiver as he turned to glance back at his young companion.

Cedric thought that Dec had fallen asleep in the saddle, but peering more closely revealed that the young man only stared down into the gauzy whiteness with despondent eyes. The knight hoped that the two might find lodging for the night, or at least a cave or some natural outcropping of rocks that might provide some shelter and allow a safe fire to be built.

"Have you been this way before?" Cedric asked in a strong voice.

There was no answer, and Cedric stopped his horse and waited for the young mage's mount to catch up. Reaching out with a light hand, the old knight touched Dec's shoulder.

The mage started so violently that he toppled over in the saddle and only saved himself from hitting the ground by grabbing onto the saddle strap. His save wasn't complete, however; the saddle slowly rotated around the barrel chest of the mount and deposited Dec on the fog-shrouded ground.

There was a small period of time where Cedric could not see his companion, causing him to entertain the notion that the boy had been swallowed by the mists. But Dec quickly stood up, wiping away the dirt and moisture on his clothes and face.

"Why did you touch me like that?" he demanded, rubbing his hands on his robes.

"I am sorry. I thought you had taken ill."

Dec was about to spit out a sharp reply when he realized that the old knight's tone of voice held nothing but extreme sincerity. He finished wiping himself off, then put the saddle back in the correct position on his mount.

"That's all right," the young mage mumbled. "My fault."

"I'll be more careful next time," Cedric added. "I didn't know you could fall asleep in your saddle."

Dec laughed at himself. "Asleep? I didn't even know!"

Cedric smiled in return. Reaching behind into a saddlebag, he produced a small length of rope which he affixed to his saddle-horn. Maneuvering Pele near the other horse, the old knight tied the other end to Dec's saddle.

"This way even if we both fall asleep, we won't get separated."

Secretly, Dec was glad for the precaution. He had not fallen asleep, but felt unusually depressed for no reason he could discover. He had started staring into the fog, then thought of how far away his home was, how he missed his parents, even how he missed his days in school. The next thing he knew, he was falling off his horse.

Glancing more cautiously into the fog again, as if the mists might be some kind of animal that ate the spirit, the young mage probed at his own enervation, but found nothing in the way of explanation. He was unusually tired, in much the same way that he felt after performing a particularly difficult spell, or even running a league. He hoped that they would stop and rest very soon.

The two rode further into the fog as the darkness left by the setting sun continued to steal over the land. Cedric could still not recall ever having seen a fog the likes of this one, and wondered if the dragon could have anything to do with it. After all, dragons were potentially hundreds of years old and most likely very intelligent. By their very natures they were magical, and there was probably no reason why they could not learn to cast spells as did the young mage.

''Do you think the dragon could have something to do with these infernal mists?'' the old knight inquired softly.

''Infernal?'' Dec questioned, as if the question were a joke. Peering through the gloom, he saw there was no mirth in the knight's face. After a moment's consideration, he ventured, ''If the dragon could breathe fire, then it might make sense that it would live in a cold place. The Law of Opposites states that in order to achieve something, you need its reflection.''

Cedric frowned. ''You don't sound particularly convinced.''

''I'm—I don't know. It's just a guess.'' Dec looked back at his older companion, hoping to continue the conversation and keep his mind off the deathly quiet of the forest. Then suddenly he spotted a pale light in the distance.

''What's that?''

Cedric turned and immediately changed their course toward the light. After a few minutes riding, he said, ''It looks like an inn.''

''Great! After this, I really need to rest.''

The light was farther than either of the men expected, though Cedric thought that the fog might also be playing tricks with his sense of time as well as his sense of direction. They eventually discovered a path which led them to the small hostel.

The inn was two stories tall and lit from within by a fire in the hearth that Cedric could see through the window. The front room was empty, but he heard voices in another part of the building.

The old knight led the horses to a hitching post, jumping down from Pele and lashing both mounts by the bridle. Dec slowly climbed off his horse, since he was not a particularly experienced rider and he really couldn't see the ground. As the mage was removing his saddlebags, Cedric tried the front door.

"It's locked," he said in some surprise.

Dec walked up and tried the door himself. "Is this unusual?"

Cedric saw that what the boy had said about spending most of his time in study was no exaggeration. Trying the door again, he replied, "Very. An inn is supposed to welcome strangers."

The door was obviously not going to open, and Cedric knocked three times, his gauntleted hand striking the stout wood resoundingly. Dec saw that the fog was curling higher about his legs, and shuffled his feet to keep himself warm, with little success. The old knight knocked again, this time a little harder.

"What's their problem?" the young mage asked, his breath leaving his mouth as a gout of steam.

The knight shrugged, rattling his heavy armor. Unsheathing the broadsword he wore at his side, he laid into the door with the pommel. The sound echoed inside the inn, but outside the door it was swallowed up by the fog.

Cedric pulled his arm back, his anger growing with every moment, when the door opened a crack. A suspicious eye appeared beneath the line of the chain barring the door.

"What do you want?" an equally suspicious voice inquired.

"Lodging, and be quick about it!" Cedric demanded. Dec saw that the knight did not sheathe the sword.

The voice did not sound impressed. "Who are you?"

"Cedric of Penwarden. Now open up or I shall smash this door open with my bare hands!"

The door slammed shut and the mage thought that the man inside had gone to further reinforce the locks. However, the chain clattered loudly to the floor and the door swung open just long enough for the two travellers to enter.

"Have you got money?" the innkeeper asked. He was a short man, past middle age, with greying hair and a dirty beard. The leather apron he wore was stained with the old blood of animals and the scent of bad ale.

Cedric reached under his belt and produced a single gold coin. The innkeeper's eyes immediately lit up, then darkened again, turning to slits. He held out his hand for the payment, but the old knight dropped the money on the floor.

"My companion and I need shelter for the night, and our horses need tending," he said in an even and commanding voice as the coin rolled in circles on the floor. Dec was so impressed by Cedric's style that he broke into a wide grin, which he promptly covered up by pretending to cough.

The innkeeper scrabbled about on the floor until he retrieved the gold. Standing, he muttered, "We'll see to the horses in the morning. You can have the room at the top of the stairs. To the right," he added, jerking his thumb behind his shoulder. Without another look, he entered the adjoining dining room.

"This is nothing like the inn owned by Carelton," Dec said.

"Carelton?"

"A famous inn on Albion."

Cedric nodded, though he had never heard of that place. Glancing inside the dining room, he saw that there were six or seven other guests present. He figured that they must all know each other since they sat at the same table and whispered amongst themselves though they were obviously from different parts of the surrounding country, wearing different clothes. The one thing they all had in common were baleful stares.

"Go up to the room, Dec, and take our bags," he commanded, though his voice was low.

Dec grew immediately defiant. He hated being ordered around. "Why can't you do it yourself? Why should I—"

The mage's hasty words were cut off by a stern glance from the knight's dark and powerful eyes. Dec bit back the rest of his statement, grabbed the travelling bags, and went up the stairs.

Cedric entered the dining room, his body filling the doorway. He was much larger than any of these men and knew that he could easily handle them all at once, especially since he was armored and carried his broadsword. However, that did not mean these farmers and vagabonds wouldn't attempt some treachery.

"What do any of you know of this fog?" he demanded. The voice of his ancestors was strong, resounding in the large room.

For a moment, the men at the table were too stunned to talk, but then they began muttering and gesturing. Cedric could tell that they were frightened by the mysterious mists, but were attempting to mask their fear with drink and anger.

"Who cares about the fog!" the innkeeper spat. "What are you doing about the dragon, *Sir* Knight?"

"The monster killed half my sheep!"

"And all my cattle!"

Cedric did not care for the tone of the men, especially the sarcastic gibe of the innkeeper. He let the insult pass and replied, "I am gathering a band of men together to fight. Do any of you—gentlemen, wish to join?"

Every man turned away, back toward his drink or the suppressed anger in a friend's eye. The old knight's mouth twisted into a grimace of disappointment, but he had expected nothing less. Most men lacked the discipline and training to be effective in combat, but more importantly most men lacked the courage.

"Then I bid you all good evening." Cedric turned to leave the room, when out of the corner of his eye he caught one of the men making an obscene gesture. Without changing direction, he whispered, "If I were a lesser man, you would be dead."

Dec's eyes widened at the knight's last words. He grabbed the railing where he had secretly listened to the entire conversation, feeling his respect for the old knight jump a hundredfold and his need to be respected by the man increase a like amount. Peering down toward the dining room, the young mage saw Cedric's shadow approaching the doorway. He leapt back in a panic, racing into their room.

Dec listened to Cedric's armored footsteps make their way up the staircase. He pretended that he was in the middle of checking some sorcerous ingredients for freshness when the knight entered the room, ducking to avoid hitting his head.

Cedric unlashed a few of his straps, carefully lowering most of his armor to the floor. After a few moments, he had removed his outer plating and wore nothing but chain and leather. Propping the broadsword on his bed, point down, he knelt before the weapon, folded his hands, and prayed.

Attempting to make out what the knight mumbled was more difficult than Dec expected, and he caught only a few words and phrases. Most of them dealt with honoring dead ancestors, but many of them asked for bravery and the safety of companions immediate and gone. Dec felt slightly prideful; after all, he was a companion as well.

When he had finished, Cedric kissed the pommel of his sword and replaced it in its sheath, laying it down on the floor near the bed. With the sound of clattering links, he stretched out on the stiff mattress and shut his eyes.

"When you are done, try to get some sleep," he said, laying the back of his hand over his forehead. "It will be a long day tomorrow and you will need all your strength."

Dec was about to say something, good night, or thank you, but when he saw Cedric on the bed, he changed his mind. The knight appeared very old in the dim light cast by the small lamp in the room, old and tired. He turned back to his ingredients with a sigh, putting them back in their appropriate places.

He would try to do as the knight commanded. He would try to get some sleep.

Dec awoke to the sound of his own heart beating in his chest. He was bathed in sweat and could not decide if he was hot or cold.

The fog pressed against the glass of the grimy window

like a sheet of lurid gossamer. Dec stared at it for a moment in the darkness, glad that the lamp had been turned off. After a moment, his fear left him and he crawled out of bed as quietly as he could, glancing at the somber form of Cedric. The young mage could not find a reason for his sudden bravery.

Dec grabbed the lamp from the table, along with a tinderbox, and made his way out the door, closing it softly behind him. The rest of the inn had finally gone to sleep, leaving the lodge in darkness. The mage's eyes quickly adapted to the lack of light and he decided not to fire the lamp.

At the bottom of the staircase, Dec had the sudden urge to go outside, and found to his surprise that his feet were leading him toward the front door. He wanted the fear to return so he could run away, back to the safety of his bed and the aegis of Sir Cedric, but his heart maintained its even rhythm and he was forced forward.

When he was within arm's reach of the door, he waved his hands in a complex series of motions, right under left, left's fingers outspread, right's together, then clenched in a fist. The counterspell drained some of his constitution but seemed to award him some of his senses back. He knew that it might have done nothing more than bolster his confidence.

He turned back from the door and decided to get some water from the dining room. He took the first steps without incident, but a few feet later he felt a great nausea take him and he doubled over, propping himself against the doorway.

There was nothing that the young mage could remember that would make him feel this way, as if his insides were being twisted around a demonic finger. He made the counterspell again, adding a sign that he himself had created, and that seemed to remove some of the agony. But his strength was waning from the exertion of sorcery, more than it should.

He was determined not to give in to his fear or his fatigue. Standing as straight as his pain would allow, he thought about the fortitude that Cedric must have shown in the face of the dragon and used that as an example to himself. Pride was the only thing that helped him reach the entrance to the dining room.

Without warning, the front door blew open, allowing a cold wind to enter the inn, though the fog remained outside, a billowing wall. Dec turned in terror. He could see nothing except for the vague haze of the crescent moon in the sky, but slowly, as his eyes adjusted to the new gloom, he made out the image of a woman, a beckoning woman with pale skin and beautiful eyes. . . .

The sun was hidden the next morning by clouds that boded ill. A storm was approaching. Cedric rose from his light sleep and rubbed some of the night's lethargy from his eyes. He looked over to his young companion to see if the boy had awakened. His bed was empty.

Dec was slumped over in front of the door, blocking the entrance with his body. His eyes held the same despondent look that they'd had while he was riding through the forest. It appeared to the old knight that the mage was half-asleep, yet aware.

Walking as softly as he could manage, Cedric leaned over and waved his hands in front of Dec's eyes. There was no response.

"Master Dec?" the knight whispered softly, touching the boy's cloaked shoulder.

Dec jerked in terror, then blinked his eyes, as if unbelieving of what he saw.

"Sir Cedric? What am I doing here?" the young mage inquired in a voice that to him sounded very far away.

Cedric helped the mage gently to his feet, maneuvering him to a sitting position on the bed. "What is the last thing you remember?" he asked.

The magician shook his head and found that he was unsure. He grasped for some words and finally replied, "A dream. A woman. A beautiful woman."

"What about this woman?"

"She wanted to kill me."

Chapter 5

THE CARAVAN AT THE COAST FOUND NOTHING, AND JAEME COULD not decide what action to take. After consulting with his counselors, he followed the advice of Alavay and left some of the men at the shore to continue the search for the ships while he returned to Castle Elfwood with the others. Jaeme was happy to do this, as Laela's condition had not improved.

The ride back was the same as the ride out, the sun hanging dead in the dark sky and the fog choking the earth. The only sounds were the clattering of pans against pots and the squeal of the wagon wheels, but even they were muted. The young lord looked back at those who followed and saw that they were all downcast, staring into the shifting mists. The unending fog, coupled with their failure to locate the ships, had dispirited everyone.

Jaeme tried to imagine what his father would have done in this situation. He pictured his father's comforting face, and for some reason his hands, but he could not summon up the voice. Blinking rapidly, the young knight found that he was staring into the rampart of fog. He shook his head to clear it and wiped his brown hair out of his eyes.

A glance at the druidess revealed that she no longer shook with chill as much as she had before, as if the trip back toward the castle and creature comforts made her feel better. Her head lolled back against one of the wagon's vertical braces, splaying the lustrous red hair out like a halo of fire. Jaeme had the urge to touch the strands, but he turned back to the reins and the problem at hand, gritting his teeth in frustration.

Sometime later, what remained of the original caravan passed through the huge outer gates of Castle Elfwood. Jaeme was in many ways glad to be back inside the ancient confines, though he knew that he still had to solve the problem of the missing vessels. If the ships could not be located, he would have to find another way to stockpile food and supplies for the winter.

Laela's eyes immediately sprang open when she passed through the gate, and Jaeme, peering inside the wagon, saw that she glanced around like someone awakening from a dream.

"What's the matter?" he asked softly, guiding the wagon into the center of the castle proper.

The druidess shook her head in confusion. "I dreamed I was cold."

Jaeme said nothing to this. He figured that whatever sickness had possessed her had affected her senses. She was better now, and that was all that mattered.

"Jaeme, why doesn't the fog come in?" Laela continued, coming up to where Jaeme sat, and looking back at the gates.

The young lord brought the wagon to a halt and turned around, hanging onto the seat so he would not fall off. As the druidess had noticed, the mists were not entering the castle proper, and not even the smallest tendril penetrated the perimeter created by the high outer walls. He felt a mix of both fear and security.

"Where is Dec when you need him?" he asked rhetorically. Jaeme was positive the mystery of this encompassing fog could be solved by the mage.

"I still don't know where this stuff is coming from," Dec answered, pressing his nose against the dining room window. Though he knew his actions must look like those of a small, curios child, he was actually testing the temperature outside. The tip of his nose was particularly sensitive.

Cedric looked at his food complacently, trying to figure out the best strategy for hiring soldiers to fight the dragon. There were some towns to the north that might prove advantageous, or if he became desperate enough, he could head further north, toward the Franks. He prodded his packed traveling bags with an armored foot.

"The dragon," he muttered to himself with a sigh. This was going to be a glorious battle, but it would not last long without proper preparation.

When Dec heard the old knight say something about the dragon, it occurred to him that he had changed his original theory. A smothering fog was not known to be one of the standard abilities of dragonhood, natural or magically induced. Rubbing his nose to get it warm again, he decided that it must be another force. Of course, there would be no harm in getting a close look at the monster.

Suddenly, Cedric pushed his chair back from the table and stood. "Let us go, Master Dec," he commanded in his shattering voice.

The innkeeper and patrons of the inn exchanged glances of relief that did not escape either the eyes of the old knight or the young mage. Neither the man nor the boy could fully understand the grudge these peasants held, but they saw no reason to tolerate them any longer.

However, Dec was a little fearful of leaving, and he glanced at the front door with trepidation. The dream from last night had seemed very real, and the woman might still be out there, waiting for him. He found that he was staring at the fog again through the panes of glass.

Cedric grabbed the mage by the arm and helped him toward the door, saying, "You said last night it was nothing more than a dream. The journey through the cold made you so tired you lost your senses.''

''But I cast *spells*,'' Dec replied quietly, attempting to dig his heels into the floorboards. Cedric was much too strong for the young man to resist. The mage stopped his futile efforts.

''How do you know what you did in your sleep?'' the knight hissed through his dark beard. Dec broke free of the man's grasp and stood silent for a moment, considering the words. In fact, there was no way for him to know exactly what he did in his sleep. He'd been taught that dreams can sometimes mirror reality so well that the dreamer cannot tell one from the other. If that were the case, then he just might be tired from the ride, like Cedric suggested, and that was all.

And if there were some other explanation, the solution would probably come too late.

The young mage looked up into his wise companion's dark eyes and said, ''All right. Let's go.''

Dec did not die when he stepped out the door, for which he was extremely grateful. This gave him renewed confidence in Cedric's decisions. He had no fear as they mounted their horses.

However, as in the dream, the fog had not entered the inn, either through the doorway or any other entrance. Coming from the college of magic, Dec assumed that his dream must have been predictive in nature, though he had never had such an experience before. His instructor at the Magisterium Lundinium once gave a lesson on the developing powers of new mages and the divergences they could take. Dec had hoped to be an evoker, though it seemed his abilities tended toward thaumaturgy. He recalled wistfully that one of the boys had been a diviner with traces of conjuration, who had been very adept at passing tests; he had kept his predictive skills a secret.

''What are you thinking about?'' Cedric asked softly, his voice barely breaking over the waves of fog.

For a moment, Dec did not hear the words, but then they

slowly registered in his mind. He silently cursed the mists because they made him continually introspective and depressed.

"Nothing. Just school."

"What is your experience with the college of magicians?" Cedric continued. He had his mind on gathering his force, but he wanted to keep the young mage awake and aware for the journey. The knight felt the stultifying effects of the fog, too, but he did not allow himself to think of his ancestors, or the names of lovers that might have been . . .

For the first time, Dec felt ashamed of the way he had treated his friends at the Magisterium, especially the teacher who had prevented his dismissal from the college. His mother and father had been so proud when he was accepted, but he had been thrown out of every other school before that, for "poor attitude," "underachieving," "dangerous pranks," and dozens of other reasons. Cedric had asked about life at the schools and the young mage wanted to impress his new friend. All he had to give was accounts of mischief.

He attempted to stammer an answer, but nothing coherent passed his lips. He hoped the old knight would not press the issue.

"I once knew a lad who set fire to the sheets of our lord's castle as a joke, and after his restitution, proceeded to remove support pegs from the beds of every officer in the barracks," Cedric said in an even tone, without looking back at his young friend.

Dec stared at the knight's back in silence, wondering if the point of the story was that Cedric had not been the most perfect of knights, as he apparently was now. The mage realized that moral lessons had never been his strong suit, but he was not necessarily blind when he ran across them.

"What was the name of this rogue?" he inquired slyly.

Cedric shrugged, his heavy armor rattling. "I don't remember. He did not last long at the castle."

Dec wanted to laugh out loud at the subtle mirth of the story, for tricking him into thinking the boy in question had been Cedric. He searched through his memories of school for a similar story, finding none.

The other boys reminded him of Jaeme and Laela, who he figured must be wondering where he and Cedric had gone. He would not have left in such a hurry, and without warning, if he hadn't had the opportunity to leave with the old knight, and if the druidess hadn't kicked him. Though he never admitted it to anyone, he felt a subtle rivalry between himself and the woman; they were both spellcasters, though the source of her abilities was different than his. Still, she could do some things that he had never considered, let alone attempted, such as changing himself into an animal. He had heard stories about one student who turned himself into a monkey and could not change back.

Jaeme was now ruler of Castle Elfwood and the surrounding lands. Not that Dec had any interest in politics. It just annoyed him that someone who was about his age could attain such a high position so quickly. Additionally, it seemed to Dec that Laela preferred the lord to him. For the first time, the mage found he was jealous.

Dec shook his head to clear these thoughts away. Jaeme and Laela were first and foremost his friends, and he should have told them where he was heading, or at least left a note. He thought about attempting a *Distat Communicatia* cantrip when Cedric called to make camp.

"Hold!" the knight called, raising his right hand. Dec's heart suddenly beat faster with panic. Anything that would make Cedric stop was most likely extremely dangerous.

"What is it?" Dec whispered, guiding his horse near Pele.

Cedric sniffed loudly at the air. "Don't you smell it?" he asked, keeping his voice low as well.

Dec closed his eyes and let his senses roam, as he had been taught in school. Mostly he smelled the cold of the fog, and behind that there was the subtlety of the woods themselves, trees, dirt, flowers . . . .

And sulphur! His eyes widened and he scrabbled about under his cloak for some key-ingredient pouches.

Cedric dismounted quietly, gesturing for the mage to do

the same; Dec did not see the knight's action at first because he was still fumbling for his equipment. When they were both finally on the ground, they stalked forward, keeping their bodies low and crouched.

It did not take long for them to find the source of the sulphur. The dragon was curled up in a clearing in the middle of a copse, plumes of acrid smoke rising from its nostrils. Cedric saw that its eyes were closed, and as before, it was curled around the corpses of dozens of dead animals.

"What do we do?" Dec hissed, choking off his words because he thought he was being too loud.

Cedric considered attacking, but he had no lance, and there wasn't enough room to mount a proper charge. He could engage the monster with his two-handed sword, but he would need a squire to assist him in changing weapons and shield, and Dec had obviously never trained in combat. From experience, he knew that his broadsword had very little chance of killing.

"We do nothing," he spat. With careful movements, Cedric guided the mage back through the woods to the horses.

"I could try to cast a spell," Dec said, juggling his components with shaking hands. Cedric watched as the young mage dropped most of his little bags, and then the rest when he bent over to pick up the first. "Maybe an *Animae Influxia*, or *Conflagras Corona*, or—"

Dec cut himself off. He realized that there was nothing he could do to harm the dragon, or even lend the slightest protection against it. He did not need to cast spells of detection to know that the monster could breathe fire and fly. It was obvious, both from sight and from Cedric's story, that the serpent's scales could protect it from any attack. The young mage doubted that even the Dean of the Magisterium Lundinium could vanquish this beast.

Putting his goods back under his cloak, Dec mounted his steed without another word. Cedric followed suit, staring back toward the clearing. As before, the fog did not come near the monster, and he could not for the life of him understand why.

The old knight took a course that maneuvered them around the clearing and the beast sleeping within. He was not pleased with his record of dealing with the beast, but knew there was nothing he could do at the moment.

He hoped that the ghosts of his ancestors were not watching.

Chapter 6

JAEME THREW THREE PILLOWS IN RAPID SUCCESSION AT THE DOOR OF Dec's apartment in the east tower of the castle. His anger was so great that he considered overturning the magician's small desk, but then decided that control was the better part of a lord's life. He sat down heavily on Dec's bed and rested his head in his hands.

Though the servants had found no evidence of the mage's departure, such as a note, Jaeme couldn't believe that Dec would leave without saying a word. The young lord figured that the servants had simply missed whatever the mage had left behind. Unfortunately, Jaeme found nothing; he even considered treachery on the part of the old knight, Sir Cedric, but immediately felt ashamed of himself. Every fibre of the man's being embodied nobility and honor to an extreme degree.

It was obvious the knight and the mage had gone off together in search of the dragon and the means to fight it. Jaeme was no longer sure why he had over doubted the old knight's words. He made the excuse to himself that the harvest was too important to overlook for any reason, but something in the back of his mind, perhaps the voice of his dead father, said that he had been afraid to admit the existence of such a creature.

Jaeme suddenly felt very angry with himself, and slammed his fists down on the bed so hard that his right hand bled. He wiped the blood onto the shirt of punishment, creating an ugly black stain on the satiny material.

"Another lesson," he muttered to himself in disgust. He walked to the only window in the room and leaned out, staring hotly into the mist-shrouded land, and imagined what would happen to his people if he did not take action against the monster. He clenched his fists until the muscles ached.

The young lord would have gone on with his self-punishment, but he stopped in surprise when he saw a large caravan slowly emerge from the mists. The wagons were long and black, moving like objects encountered in a dream, or more precisely, a nightmare. They did not seem to be headed in any particular direction.

Glancing down, he saw that there were guards and other workers on duty near the gates, preparing to meet the visitors, as well as stablehands and others meandering toward the entrance. Jaeme could understand the reluctance of the people to leave the castle. Although the fog that caused such strange chills and depression would not enter, it continued to form just outside the walls.

With a last look around the room for the missing note, Jaeme replaced everything the way he had found it, tossing the pillows back on the bed before leaving. He shut and locked the door behind him with the master key. He felt very tired since he had been awake the whole night with his counselors, trying to find a solution to the problem of the missing ships. They were as much at a loss as he, and only gave advice that he had already considered.

However, if he was about to have guests, he would have to make himself look presentable. He began the trek back to his chambers on the other side of the keep. The walls he passed were all familiar, and he was sure that he could remember every rough and smooth stone that he had ever run his hand across as a child. But now, with new responsibility, he saw the stones with a certain feeling of detachment, as if they were no longer merely stones but something it was his duty to protect.

That feeling increased when he ran across a small group of servants' children running through the halls. They were as happy as the mists would allow and their parents permit, and most of all they were part of the castle that was Jaeme's home and stead. For a moment he battled against his own will and fatigue to give in to his enervation. His fortitude easily won out and he continued his steps with the same determination he'd brought to the knights' testing ground.

Jaeme made his way to his quarters and stopped outside to listen at the thick oak door. He did not hear anything except for the occasional sound of glass touching glass. Knocking twice, he turned the handle and slowly opened the door.

Laela stared out toward the castle's main gate. It seemed to Jaeme that she wore more fur than a bear, and the half-full pot boiling in the fire meant that her chills had returned. The young lord stared at the woman's back and waited for the druidess to turn around, since he did not want to startle her.

Laela heard Jaeme enter the room, but could not tear her mesmerized gaze away from the reptilian line of the black wagons. She had never before seen or heard of anything like them. What bothered her most was an accompanying sense of foreboding that she could not identify.

"Whose wagons are those?" she whispered without turning around.

Jaeme did not answer at first because he was not sure he heard the question. He had been staring at Laela's halo of red hair and wondering how much like silk it must feel. After a moment he realized that she was talking.

"What?"

"Whose wagons are those?" the druidess repeated, turning around. She felt Jaeme's gaze lock with hers, and she felt for him what she knew he was feeling for her. Out of respect for her mission, however, she believed that she should not become personally involved beyond the level of what was required to fulfill her assignment. Where the young lord was concerned, she found it difficult to maintain this vigil.

Jaeme broke the contact first, walking to an open wardrobe and shuffling through its contents for something fresh to wear. After some consideration, he decided on simple black clothing, but remembered how garish the shirt of punishment would look underneath; sighing, he nevertheless took the black outfit into the adjoining lavatory, where he could change in privacy.

When he emerged, making sure that the ensemble included a belt to hang a sword, he replied to Laela's questions. "I don't know who the wagons belong to. I don't think they were flying any flags."

"Was your . . . was your father expecting any guests he didn't tell you about?" Laela asked, stammering over the first words. Though he never mentioned it, it was obvious to her that Jaeme missed his father dearly.

The young lord appreciated the druidess's candor. "Not that he told me. And if there were, one of the counselors would probably know, and they never mentioned anything either."

There was a hail of greeting from outside, and Jaeme and Laela both rushed to look out the window, thinking that the caravan had gained the gate. However, the wagons cutting through the mists were still a good distance away and only a lone rider appeared.

"That's Joseph!" Jaeme exclaimed. Leaning out the window, he shouted, "Joseph! Joseph! What news?"

The new lord's friend yelled something, but Jaeme could not hear. Joseph gestured for him to come down.

"He looks frantic," Laela observed. Being so near the window gave her the shivers again, which she now realized had stopped when Jaeme entered the room.

Jaeme nodded agreement. "Will you come down with me?"

Laela took his proffered hand.

* * *

"You wouldn't believe these ships," Joseph said, almost shouting. He was very hot from the ride, despite the clutching cold.

"What about them?" Jaeme asked as his friend rubbed down his tired horse with a heavy brush.

Joseph replied, "There were—it looked like they were a hundred years old."

"What? What are you talking about?"

"No, really," the other knight insisted, finally turning from his task. "The hulls were rotted through and what was left of the sails crumbled to dust when we touched them."

Laela could not understand how such a thing could have happened. "Are you sure you had the right ships?"

Joseph shrugged. "They had all the correct supplies, all the food and materials for the winter."

"Then everything was still there," Jaeme stated with a smile; the situation was not as hopeless as he thought.

"No. All that was rotted as well."

Jaeme became very disturbed. This meant that the winter's surplus would have to come from a different quarter, assuming it would actually be needed. He knew there was always the chance that the countryside would not require any more food than could be harvested before the winter, but the surrounding ramparts of heavy fog and the accompanying cold did not bode well.

"Laela, is there anything to your knowledge that could cause such a thing?" Jaeme inquired. He thought that perhaps a different, more magical approach, might offer a solution to the mystery.

The druidess thought back through her teachings under Myrna, who had been a mother to her when Laela's real parents had died. Unlike the mystical cantrips of Dec and other magicians, a druid's power lies within the strength of the land and little more. The information about the ships was something she'd never heard about.

She was not going to give up, though. "Was there anything else about the ships?"

"Were they taking on water?" Jaeme added with sudden inspiration.

Joseph stared off into the fog a moment, the emotion on his face dropping visibly to his two friends. "Yes, you're right. The ships were leaking. Through a lot of fist-sized holes," he said, holding up a fist.

The information helped neither Jaeme nor Laela. With a heavy sigh, the new lord of Elfwood kneaded his forehead with his hands. There was nothing he could do about the vessels now.

"Send the ships to sea and scuttle them. We don't want them—"

Suddenly, something very basic made itself evident in Jaeme's thoughts. There was a fact they were all overlooking in their confusion. Meeting Laela's glance, the young lord saw that she now understood as well.

"What about the crew?" he inquired, slightly fearful for reasons he could not identify.

"The crew?" Joseph asked, as if awaking from a disturbing dream. "They were missing."

"We should return to Penwarden," Cedric said, ducking under a branch as he led Pele through a twist of brambles. His temper was short, and the memory of leaving the dragon without a battle disturbed him.

Dec could hear the repressed anger in his companion's voice; he guessed that knights didn't like to leave something like a dragon unvanquished, or at least that Cedric, the epitome of knighthood, did not. However, the first evening in Castle Elfwood, Cedric had mentioned that he would not receive any more aid from Penwarden. The young mage guessed that the knight was becoming desperate, and that was making him forget his own words.

"I don't think that would be a good idea," Dec said, biting his lower lip in anticipation of the knight's response.

Cedric was inflamed by the comment. "And why is that, *Master* Dec?"

"Elfwood has more men, more supplies, and more lines of communication to the surrounding lords," the young mage replied. He stopped walking his horse for a moment to regain his lost confidence. "And Elfwood has something none of the other castles can boast."

"And that is?"

"A magician and a druid," Dec answered.

Cedric ran his hands across his face, batting away at the cloying fog as if it were a cloud of insects. He had let his anger get the better of him, and Dec certainly did not deserve this kind of behavior. "Please excuse me, Dec," he said slowly, liberating his ire with every word. "There is much of me you do not know."

Dec moved closer to the knight and almost put his hand on the large man's armored shoulder. Stopping himself with embarrassment, he replied, "That's all right. I can say the same thing."

The two continued to walk their horses through the tangled undergrowth until they came upon a thin stream that ran north. Dec realized that the only reason they found it was because the water continued to splash against the small, flat rocks, making a sound that was not quite squelched by the cold mists. After a brief consideration, Cedric decided that they should head upstream to hopefully run across a main road.

As they marched, Dec tried to find the source of his nightmare of the beautiful woman. He still could not understand why she wanted to kill him; actually, he wasn't sure that *kill* was the correct word. Perhaps *devour*, or even *possess*. He shook his head in confusion and patted his horse's neck for comfort. Somehow, he was afraid that he might dream of her again.

After what seemed like hours later to the two companions, they finally came across a road, apparently well-used from the number of wagon-gutters, horse-tracks, and footprints gouged into the damp earth. Cedric bent down and touched the ground with his fingers where a cart had been pulled, and Dec had the idea that the knight was using some kind of tracking skill.

"These people were leaving together, an exodus," Cedric muttered.

"Why do you say that?"

The old knight pointed to the wheel-tracks. "This cart is like that one there. They are too narrow to be used for anything but light loads, but the depth of the gutters they created suggests they carried an incredible weight."

Dec shrugged. "Couldn't the dirt just be loose?"

Cedric considered that, but the earth in the few places near the roadside where nothing had travelled was reasonably hard. "There are too many of these tracks that are too fresh."

Bending down on one knee, Dec waited for the fog to clear slightly so he might observe the ground. After a moment, he saw that not only were there many overloaded wagons, but that men, women, and children must all have been moving. "It looks like everyone packed up their families to go. What would make them do that?"

"The dragon?" Cedric suggested. He hoped the monster had not caused any harm. If it had, he would not forgive himself for leaving the beast.

"I don't know anything about dragons," Dec began, formulating an answer, "but I doubt that a dragon would *drive* people from their homes. Wouldn't it just kill them or eat them or something?"

Cedric pondered his young friend's words and found them sound, though he, too, knew little of the ways of dragons. "You could be right, but something must have made these people flee."

Dec made his voice strong. "Then let's move back up the road and find out."

With a nod, Cedric mounted his horse and pointed for Dec to do the same. The old knight was happy that the mage had made the suggestion to investigate. He doubted that any of the "knights" in Penwarden would have offered to do the same.

The village was mostly deserted, and the few peasants who remained had taken refuge near the central cluster of buildings. The town reminded Dec of many of the older and smaller villages in the country on the island that his parents had taken him to visit.

Something that the young mage noticed that he was not sure his companion would see was that the fog rolled in wherever it pleased, moistening walls and putting a sheen on every piece of wood, tree, and tool. It even cascaded over the huge bonfire the people had set in the middle of the town, huge waves of fog that would not dissipate.

Pele shied away from the fire, but Cedric did not think the horse was afraid of anything so mundane. Approaching, he saw that the peasants huddled in small groups, whispering amongst themselves and staring out into the woods with baleful glances. When the horse whinnied once, everyone turned to stare at the two strange men coming in out of the mists. The old knight saw more than one sword or scythe prepared for combat. It was obvious this was a town gripped in fear, one that Cedric did not relish the idea of entering.

Cedric decided to get off his horse, though he was reluctant to give up the advantage of his superior height when mounted. He knew there were times when a strong voice and a show of peaceful intentions could rule the day instead of the iron hand of force.

"Who are you?" a man called out from the largest group of peasants, stepping boldly into the wan firelight. Dec could tell from his own experience studying for exams that the man had not slept well in many days, if he had slept at all.

"I am Sir Cedric of Penwarden, and this is Decutonius Consulus, from Albion."

The name Penwarden sent a ripple of angry mutters through the crowd. Cedric was confused by the many disrespectful remarks made of Lord Penwarden, especially in regard to matters like taxes.

"I am the mayor of this village. What do you want?" the man inquired of Cedric, holding his hand up for silence from the crowd. His voice was harsh and his eyes suspicious.

"We are gathering men to fight the dragon," Cedric said in a voice that shook the trees.

The word "dragon" raced like fire through the huddled peasants, but it died out with cries for lost mothers, fathers, and children. Dec, who had maintained his distance from Cedric so the knight could look more impressive, edged closer.

"They don't seem particularly concerned with the dragon," he whispered out of the corner of his mouth.

Cedric nodded in confirmation but did not say anything. He heard more talk about missing loved ones, and some about the fog.

"We don't need your help here, *Sir* Knight," the mayor said with a sneer. "Nobody came to our rescue when our families disappeared into the fog."

"What are you talking about?" Cedric demanded. "When did your families vanish?"

"When the fog came!" an old woman yelled, stepping bravely into the open. She shook her fist in the air with a silent curse.

Dec and Cedric glanced at each other a moment. Neither could make any connection between the fog and the dragon. However, Dec wondered if there was still a connection to make.

"Perhaps if you tell me more, I can—" the old knight began amiably, holding out his hands in a gesture of peace.

"I think you'd best be leaving," the mayor said.

From behind, Dec heard the snap of a crossbow being loaded and the drawing of several swords. He saw Cedric stiffen in response. Dec was glad he could not see the knight's dark eyes.

Cedric turned and remounted his horse, and Dec scrambled to do the same. With a final furious glance, Cedric turned Pele around and moved out toward the edge of town.

"Get them!" the mayor yelled. Dec heard the crossbow release its bolt, but his mind was on other things. Reaching under his pouch, he pulled out a pinch of sulphur and three ash twigs he had prepared with oil.

"*Pedium Excelsium—*"

A great sheet of fire appeared behind the two horses and moved like a wave toward the center of the village. The roar of the flames was like a thousand men. The townspeople cried out in panic.

Satisfied that his actually very simple spell had worked, Dec hunched down low on his horse and dug his heels into its flanks. He wanted to turn to see the results, which from such a minor cantrip would be nothing more than singed hair, but he greatly preferred to get out of the village with his life.

Through the fog and the rising dust, Cedric rode close beside him. Dec glanced at his companion once, expecting to see approval, but the old knight's eyes blazed with more fury than the magical fire. They spoke of old prejudice.

There were more shouts from behind, but they quickly receded behind the sound of pounding hooves. After a time of fast riding, the two slowed to a trot, then finally halted.

Dec felt tired, and he found his breathing was hard and deep. "Do you think they'll follow?"

"Undoubtedly. They know this area better than we."

The young mage heard the cold words. They froze his spirit more than the fog. However, he could not bring himself to any defense because he suddenly felt very dizzy.

"Cedric, I—"

Dec fell into Cedric's arms. The magician saw that the knight's face betrayed panic. Then he lost consciousness.

Cedric gently laid Dec down onto the soft earth, removing a blanket from his riding bag and placing it over the magician for warmth. He was careful not to shift the crossbow bolt that had viciously bitten into Dec's shoulder.

Glancing back the way they had come, he removed his knife, flint, and steel, and prepared himself for the arduous task ahead.

Chapter 7

THE NIGHT WAS FILLED WITH NOTHING BUT TROUBLING HALF-dreams and restlessness for Jaeme. He knew that if he did not get some proper rest soon, he would be unable to function as a person, let alone the lord of a castle.

Slipping quietly out of bed, Jaeme walked to the window and stared out. The sun would be rising soon, though he did not think the life-giving light would be able to touch the land. He found that the idea of the black caravan near Elfwood made him uneasy. They had not called upon the castle. There was no reason for this that he could discover, and it made him think that his lack of sleep was making him fear everything. Even the fog was beginning to drown his hopes and make him doubt himself.

The half-dream that troubled him most was that of his father, reaching out and holding the jewel-hilted sword rumored to be magicked. Jaeme had been given the weapon upon Richard's death, and told of its potential power. But he had yet to test its ability, preferring to keep the blade in its sheath and hanging in the Great Hall as a reminder of a once-great man. He wondered why he had not thought about it until now.

The sun would be rising soon, and the young lord's thoughts went to Laela, who was sleeping in another part of the castle in airy chambers she herself had chosen. She had planted her own garden outside her window in hanging planters, all of which were filled with the most exotic array of spices and herbs Jaeme had ever seen. She had told him that they were medicinal and druidical uses. He wondered if there were something there that might help him sleep.

There was, he knew, another reason for his thinking about the red-haired woman, but he refused to give it serious consideration. To entertain ideas of courting her would be ridiculous.

Frustrated and angry at everything he could think of, Jaeme tore off his nightclothes and stormed to his closet. He removed a pair of simple leather pants and a matching jacket, donning both. The shirt of punishment appeared deeply black in the night.

The young lord left the room, closing the door quietly behind him. He decided to walk the castle walls for some fresh air, hoping it might make him less apprehensive and restless. As he left his room and advanced down the hallway that led to the rest of the castle, his thoughts returned to the liquid dreams of his father and the sword, its jewels aglitter in his hand when he first drew it from the sheath. He let his steps take him toward the Great Hall, a considerable walk away, his mind drifting.

Jaeme's need for Dec surfaced again from within his inner turmoil. The mage could have been some help in discovering the reason for the demise of the supply ships, but he was gone, as was the knight from Penwarden. Sighing heavily, Jaeme hoped that whatever they were doing, they were safe.

The Great hall was deserted, though the torches in their holders were always lit. The flickering lights cast baleful shadows against the walls, which reminded Jaeme of the rolling ramparts of fog outside the castle walls. The sight made his heart race with fear, bringing back the question of what befell the sailing ships.

The magic sword given to him by his father hung in its place above the coat of arms of the Mortimer family. He had not taken the sword from its place since the fight with Talvice, the mercenary who had taken Castle Elfwood and would have brought about its destruction if not for the help of the Druidic Council and a spell cast by Dec. Without fully realizing what he was doing, Jaeme pushed a chair under the heraldic shield and pulled down the weapon. The instant he touched the silver sheath, he felt a great peace come over him and all his questions faded. The anguish he felt for his father abated slightly as well, and he once again pictured Richard's face and reaching hands.

With a sigh, Jaeme stepped down from the chair and turned to face the Great Hall. The weight on his shoulders had suddenly become much lighter. The problems he'd been facing for the past nights no longer seemed to be as important as other matters, matters that could be resolved immediately.

The young lord replaced the chair and walked out of the Great Hall with strong steps. He still felt fatigued from lack of sleep, but his thoughts were clear as he strapped on the sword by its light silver chains. The weapon was almost weightless on his hip.

In the main hallway, the guards he passed saluted, and he returned the gestures. He noticed, under their partial helmets, ill-concealed looks of consternation, which worried him. They obviously felt threatened by something, and if the lord of the castle was not going to do anything about it, perhaps they would take matters into their own hands. Putting his hand on the smooth hilt of the sword, he told himself to ask Desmond about the condition of the soldiers. He guessed that Cedric would do the same, and that boosted his confidence.

The air outside was bitterly cold, and Jaeme wished that he had worn something heavier. The fog continued its roiling outside the confines of the wall, weakly illuminated by torches hung in the walls for the night-watch's safety. He could see that like the guards inside, the watchmen on the walls were nervous, talking softly amongst themselves in small groups. They constantly gestured toward the pale mists, and Jaeme saw that the routes they chose to walk kept them as far away from the choking wisps as possible. As he arrived at the gate, he wished desperately that Dec was in the castle to help solve this mystery as well as that of the ships.

Jaeme saw that the caravan was still parked outside the castle's walls. The horses at the fore of the wagons were all perfectly black and difficult to discern in the dark and fog. They appeared to the young lord as unmoving ethereal shapes. He listened for the sounds of the labored breathing of horses, or even an occasional hoof pawing the earth, but all that was audible were the sounds of the castle, a baby crying, guards shifting weapons.

Jaeme put his hand back on the hilt of his sword. When he'd taken the weapon from the wall, he had decided to overcome the first and most immediate of his problems, that of the mysterious black caravan. But now that he was in front of the strange wagons, he was not sure of his next course of action. There appeared to be about twenty in the train, all as dark as the horses that pulled them.

"Let's go," Jaeme commanded himself. His voice sounded small and reedy in the gloom, but he was not ashamed. Though he felt some trepidation about leaving the apparent safety of the castle and walking into the rampart of fog, he did not falter in his resolve.

He had expected some kind of stultifying sensation when his skin touched the mists, but there was nothing more than the same cold he felt in the castle air. He thought it odd that this increased his confidence.

His first close-up look at the caravan, however, set him back considerably. As Jaeme approached the first wagon, he saw that it appeared to be indescribably old, so old that it outdated even the great wall built by Offa Sarcassm. Unlike the wall, the train's age was a heavy and stifling weight, seeming to mimic the effect of the fog in wood and iron.

Each wagon was pulled by three of the largest horses

Jaeme had ever seen, larger than even Sir Cedric's steed by several hands. They kept their heads bent toward the ground. Jaeme looked for a sign of their breath in the air, but found nothing. To him it seemed that they might be black statues.

The wagon Jaeme approached was the size of a small cottage, carried on a ragged frame of knotted wood and rolled on iron-banded wheels that reached up to his throat. The wagon's canopy was protected by a field of old iron plates, interlaced like the scales of some great, black serpent, bolted to the structure hidden beneath. There were no seats for drivers and no reins on the animals.

The new Lord of Elfwood reached out to touch the side of the wagon, but could not bear to feel what he knew must be the cold of old iron that had seen more winters than the oldest man in the castle. He stood for a moment pondering the meaning of the caravan, what they wanted, where they came from. The answers that formed were shapeless and meaningless, much like the half-dreams of his sleepless nights. The idea that there were people in the wagons came only as an afterthought.

Jaeme became aware that he was completely alone with the mysterious visitors. Without turning, he could tell that there were no guards at the wall peering down into the mists, their fear having taken them to other parts of the castle. The feeling of isolation and the sensation of imminent danger grew until he thought that he would have to leave the caravan or scream.

His hand on the sword was the only comfort in the roiling mists, and with it he was able to maintain his composure and walk slowly to the back of the wagon. The frame and iron plates were replaced by a single sheet of metal, heavily bolted into place and perfectly clean and smooth. The featureless door had no handle and apparently could only be opened from the inside.

As Jaeme stepped nearer to the door, he thought about attempting to open it, or perhaps knocking, but the sound of what could have been a slamming door to his left made him stop and turn. His heart raced, and the tension was so great he thought his back would snap. He peered vainly into the fog and darkness, straining his eyes to see if one of the caravan people had left his iron confines or was returning from a nocturnal walk.

The sound's echo against the protective walls of Elfwood Castle rang in the young lord's ears, giving him a degree of fortitude. Straightening himself out, he went back to the first wagon and lifted his fist to strike the iron. . . .

The first rays of the sun slowly penetrated the choking mists, wreathing the castle in a dim halo. Jaeme looked up to the light, then back to the wagon. He wanted to know why the wagons stood before his home and dominion, but knew that there were other matters that required his attention. The caravan would have to wait, and perhaps the people within would make themselves known.

With slow, even steps, the young lord walked back to his rooms and the duties of a new day.

Dec was draped limply over the back of his horse, slowly led by Pele through the nocturnal woods. Cedric had forced the bolt through the other side of his shoulder because the tip was barbed and would have ruined the young magician's body. The old knight hoped there was no poison on the missile. If the villagers had been willing to use a weapon against an unarmed youth, they might be willing to do anything.

The fog made the trip slow and grated on Cedric's nerves. He wanted to find a place of safety so he might rest, and also a place where Dec could recover from his wounds. The damage would only start to heal in a sanctuary that had heat and food and a bed. Every step Pele took was one more moment of uncertainty for Cedric, as he truly had little idea which way to get out of the woods, let alone to a dwelling.

He heard the peasants every once in a while, far away and difficult to locate in the roiling mists, but close enough so that he halted the horses and waited in silence. He did not enjoy these games of cat and mouse, moving, stopping, moving again, forced by sounds that echoed and played in the fog. Cedric remembered a time when he'd been forced by a rout to skulk in the smoke of a burning forest for so long that he coughed black corruption from his lungs for over a year. He had been with a contingent of men who either succumbed to the choking clouds or gave into despair and surrendered.

Something loud and metallic dropped against wood in the distance, forcing Cedric to pull back lightly on the reins of the horses. He realized that he had been unconsciously hunching down low in the saddle and holding his hand to his mouth. Moving his hand away, he tasted the smoke again, black, heavy, and recalled that the men who surrendered had been butchered where they stood.

Waiting as long as he dared, Cedric rode out slowly again, tugging on Dec's horse to follow. The boy had not yet awakened, and the old knight figured it was for the best. If the dream that the mage had during their stay at the inn had been as disturbing as described, then Cedric had no doubt that any sleep would be rejuvenating and well needed.

The mists crept under Cedric's armor in ways that he never thought possible. Every piece of leather that touched his skin was so damp and cold that he thought he would have to remove the attached chain mail and replace the entire work. He had been wearing the same suit for many years, but the damage caused by the dragon was the greatest it had ever sustained. Cedric felt that the smiths at Elfwood Castle were puissant in their art and had performed an admirable job repairing the plate. Despite that, the sharp sensation in his back said that not even they could save him from having to acquire new mail.

A shimmering, remembered image of the dragon appeared in the mists, making Cedric angry and strangely despondent. In his thoughts, he had failed twice to deal effectively with the monster, and there was no telling where it might be located since he left its horrifying presence. He grated his teeth and rubbed his face with his gauntleted hands, not caring if the metal ate into his skin.

Cedric thought that stars of fatigue had formed before his eyes, but the dim light that appeared in the distance remained no matter how many times he blinked. His heart grew lighter and he felt there might be hope for some much needed rest, though more for Dec than himself. The sound of the angry peasants no longer wafted through the walls of mist, which could mean that they were far behind, or perhaps had given up the chase, though the old knight did not believe this to be true. Risking a little more speed, Cedric spurred Pele and Dec's steed on through the night.

The light came from an unusually large oil lamp in the window of a house strangely set in the middle of the woods. Cedric decided that the dwelling could possibly belong to a woodsman, or perhaps someone with a small orchard nearby. Though he found it to be very unusual, he did not ponder over it, since the mage was ailing and required an escape from the penetrating cold and gloom of the choking fog.

The house had a hitching post large enough for several horses, but Cedric saw that the ground had not been softened by hooves for quite some time. Possibly the fog had wiped away some of the more recent prints, but that did not seem likely.

"Where are we?"

The old knight turned just in time to catch Dec as he fell from the horse. The magician's eyes fluttered open, and he saw Cedric's face as soft and hospitable, actually caring. Remembering the bravery he wanted to show the old knight, he struggled to stand on his own, though his knees felt weak.

"Where are we?" he asked again. His mouth was filled with the taste of sickness, and his shoulder throbbed in time with his heart.

"Somewhere in the woods," Cedric replied, stepping closer when Dec threatened to fall over again. The mage held out his hand and steadied himself against his horse, which tossed its head and snorted in reaction.

The last thing Dec remembered was casting a spell that scattered the villagers, but he couldn't quite remember what the spell had been. He absently dug through the pouches under his robes and found that the twigs for a fire curtain were missing.

"We are lost somewhere in the woods, and the people from the village want our heads," Cedric explained patiently. "We've been searching for a place to rest."

"Why did they want to kill us?" Dec inquired, reaching up to feel his shoulder. When he touched the wound bound by one of Cedric's kerchiefs, he yelled out loud with pain. He was caught again by the old knight before hitting the ground.

Cedric put Dec's hand around his armored shoulder and walked toward the door to the house, careful not to disturb the field dressing. As they hobbled together, he said, "They said something about their families disappearing."

"Nothing about the dragon?"

The knight shook his head as they stopped in front of the door. He knocked hard three times, but received no response.

Dec was confused, and felt his thoughts begin to slip away. "This place isn't that big," he mumbled past numb lips. "They must have heard us."

Cedric knocked again, then tried the doorknob. It was locked. As carefully as he could, he rested Dec against the side of the house, ensuring that the young man would not fall, then went to the window and peered inside. There was nothing unusual to see except that the dining table was covered by plates of half-eaten food. There were three chairs

"What did you see?" Dec asked when the knight returned. His vision kept dimming and he heard the ocean in his ears.

"Nothing. There's nobody there."

The knight was torn; he did not want to force entry into another person's home. One look at the mage's failing health, however, was enough to convince him that he must overcome his scruples. Stepping back several paces, he ran into the door with his shoulder, letting the rigid plate take the blow. His arm went slightly numb from the shock, but the door did not open. He turned and went to his original position, rushing into the door again with no effect.

"I don't understand," he muttered, rubbing his shoulder. "I have splintered doors stouter than this."

"Go through the window," Dec whispered. He was quite surprised that he could say the words since the cold was so debilitating.

As he helped Dec to the window Cedric berated himself for not thinking of this himself. Making sure that the mage would be safe from any flying glass, he shattered the pane with a punch of his gauntleted hand, the armor protecting him from harm. To his confusion, he saw that the frame had been nailed shut. He ignored that for the moment, and with a few swipes of his arm the entire window was clear. He helped Dec inside.

The house was very warm and appeared well protected against the cold, retaining most of whatever heat had been made by a long-dead fire in the fireplace. Cedric assumed this would be normal since the forest was undoubtedly frozen during parts of the winter. What caught his eye was the barricade in front of the door he had tried to smash open, obviously put there to prevent the entry of something remarkably strong.

"That's very odd," he commented, scanning the rest of the room.

"What's that?" Dec asked. At first, the heat had almost made him swoon, but he felt much better now. His mind was clear of much of its lethargy.

With a gesture, Cedric replied, "They barricaded the door but left the windows unbarred."

"And if they were nailed shut and there are no other entrances, where are the owners?" Dec asked rhetorically as he sat heavily in a nearby chair. He could not answer his own question, and found that particularly disturbing.

The old knight shook his head in bewilderment. He did not know the answer to that question, either. Moving to the dinner table, he saw that the food was old, the fruits and vegetables rotting with the blackness that comes from a few day's exposure. The meat was cold and grey, and the water in the simple clay pitcher lukewarm.

With a glance at his young charge, Cedric began to climb

the stairs; Dec waved his hand in a silent gesture indicating he was fine. The stairs were sturdy, though they complained loudly under the weight of the knight's armor.

Cedric reached the top of the stairs and found nothing but a large loft with three beds and a straw mat for a dog at the foot of the smallest bed. Pursing his lips, he trudged back down the stairs, confusion showing on his face and coloring his thoughts.

"I don't understand any of this," he said to the young mage as he leaned against a nearby post.

Dec shrugged his shoulders. He had tried to ponder this mystery, but his thoughts were still too cloudy, and the pain in his shoulder had returned to give him further distraction. Leaning his head back and sighing, he strained futilely to breach the fence of confusion.

Removing his gauntlets and walking to the dining table, Cedric sat down gently on a chair. He glanced around the room again, and for a moment saw nothing of interest. Dec watched the knight's actions, and was surprised when the old knight slowly stood, an expression of curiosity strangely mixed with dread darkening his features. Cedric opened the door to the closet underneath the stairs.

"What is it?" the magician asked when the knight did not speak or move. Dec walked up and peered over Cedric's shoulder, trying to get a better look at whatever had stunned him into silence.

Cedric backed out of the cubby, holding a small child in his arms as if she were made of the most fragile glass. Dec was overcome by grief when he stared into the girl's eyes, wide with infinite fear and pain. She wrapped her arms tightly about herself as if unbearably cold.

The knight could almost feel the chill of the girl's body, even through his armor. He had never seen such anguish, and his time on battlefields could be measured in ages. He almost allowed himself to share this child's pain, but saw that the mage would need as much support as could be provided.

Dec ran to the broken window and climbed out, ignoring the flame in his shoulder. He returned a moment later with

Cedric's saddlebags and a blanket, which he spread on the floor. Using a bag for a pillow, he took the girl from the knight's embrace and placed her gently on the blanket.

"We'll need a fire," he said to Cedric. In fact, he was not sure why they would require a fire, but he felt that he needed to do something and warmth was probably an excellent start.

Without a word, Cedric removed the tinderbox from one of his bags and took an armful of wood out of the closet. He set the logs into the grate and started the fire, fanning the smoke up the chimney as best he could.

Dec noticed that the amount of smoke in the room was unusually thick and wondered why there was a problem. He took the pitcher from the table and doused the logs with water, letting the fire die with a tired hiss of steam. The mage held his breath and peered up into the chimney.

"Saints," he whispered desperately, scrambling away. Cedric saw that the mage's eyes were wide with fear and tears. Also holding his breath to avoid the remaining fumes the old knight looked into the darkness.

Cedric slowly pulled his head back, cradling his face in his hands. He had seen things that no man should ever witness, and his duty as a knight was to ensure that they would never need be seen by those of lesser strength. His training had shown him how to expunge from his mind the most horrid effects of the battlefield on flesh.

But he knew that the sight of the girl's dead parents jammed into the confining prison of the chimney would forever haunt his dreams.

Chapter 8

THE HOOVES OF THE HORSES SHOULD HAVE MADE THE SOUND OF small thunder, but Jaeme realized that the seemingly unending fog muffled the pounding. The high-collared cloak kept him reasonably warm in the unnatural cold, but he wished that he could have worn something heavier beneath his armor.

The twenty knights who rode with him had been summoned from their manors in the estates that surrounded Castle Elfwood. They owed their fealty to Richard Mortimer, who Jaeme knew had exacted oaths from each of them at one time or another during their early careers as protectors of the land. Unfortunately, the young lord did not know all the men by name or by the heraldic banners that hung from their lances and was forced to rely on the expertise and memory of Desmond, who rode nearby. The fact that the sun was little more than a memory in the sky made sighting the banners especially difficult.

Laela watched Jaeme from her steed to his right. More than the chill of the early afternoon air made her shiver as she recalled the glares of the nobles when she rode up beside their new lord. Many murmured about women being bad luck on the battlefield, and others made even less complimentary remarks, all of which the druidess had expected. In fact, she had purposely kept her distance from Jaeme so his position among the men would not be weakened. From their time together, she knew that he had no such superstitions and felt no offense.

However, Laela wondered how they would fare in this battle, especially against so powerful a creature as a dragon. She did not doubt the ability of a single knight in this retinue, the men-at-arms, or the line of archers, but the stories of the monsters had always involved some knight of especial nobility or puissance, and none of these men seemed lords of legendary note.

Another factor that worried her was Jaeme's inexperience, though she said nothing about that to him. He was sincere in his desire to rid the realm of the dragon and had relegated command to one of the oldest and most trusted knights in the kingdom, Sir Kipp; the other lords would obey his command and none other. Glancing to her left, she saw that in his saddle, his father's jeweled sword hanging at his side, Jaeme looked to be a splendid knight. She hoped that his decisions would be equally great.

Jaeme felt Laela's stare on his back but did not turn to face her. He knew that she was thinking about his lack of experience, and he harbored no illusions about his skill as a battlefield commander, especially since he continued to wear the bright shirt of punishment. He had agreed to fight the dragon because his counselor Sejanus Alavay offered indisputable arguments. Leker and Teves had been concerned, but unlike the other advisor, did not have family in the land of Penwarden, where it was said by peasants that the monster was near. The young lord would have waited for the master of Penwarden to either mount his own attack or grant aid to Castle Elfwood for its own, but he felt that there was no time for an answer. If what the farmers said was true, then the dragon would have to be killed quickly before it caused further harm.

What Jaeme would like to have had most was a magician at his side. Dec was still nowhere to be found, and Jaeme worried about the young man's safety, though he assumed that under the protection of Sir Cedric no man need fear. The new Lord of Elfwood glanced back toward his retinue, catching an occasional glimpse of colored banner through the turning mists. Despite their obvious prowess, he did not see a single man who matched the stature of Cedric.

"How much further do we need to ride?" Jaeme asked Desmond, breaking away from his grim thoughts and the monotony of the journey.

The swordmaster produced a roll of parchment from under his tunic and unfurled it. Jaeme saw that the man kept on his horse through the strength of his legs alone. "If we can maintain our pace, we should reach the grove before twilight," Desmond replied over the sound of hooves.

Jaeme waved his understanding. He did not expect that the information provided to Sejanus would be particularly accurate, as the average man did not know how to make a map or read the land beyond the immediate area of his home. He was putting a great deal of trust into what the advisor said, feeling that the number of reports that had trickled in about the dragon since the fog appeared justified such action. In many ways he hoped he was correct, as he did not want to appear gullible in the eyes of the other nobles. But he would have traded that to spare the life of a single man on this field.

From behind, Jaeme heard the sound of an approaching horse, obviously one of the knights coming up from out of the ranks to ask a question. When he turned, the young lord saw that the rider was his appointed commander.

"Good morning, Sir Kipp!" Jaeme said cheerfully, despite his inner doubts. The knight was one of the many nobles to whom he was introduced that he could remember from his childhood. He recalled that the man was tall, strong, and had an unusually ironic outlook, something another knight might consider a detriment to the cause of chivalry.

"And to you, my lord," the noble replied after lifting his visor. His face was thin and handsome, and he sported a well-groomed mustache. His hair was greying at the temples. Laela saw that the man smiled.

Desmond spurred his horse to move closer to Jaeme's, for which the young lord was grateful. He did not want to offend anyone with his inexperience of courtly manners, especially not the man who would lead Jaeme's knights into battle.

In a move that surprised both Jaeme and Laela, Sir Kipp rode closer to the young lord, neatly cutting off the trainer's approach. "Keep your distance, Desmond," the noble said amiably. "I am not as worried about the lord's manners as you."

Desmond did not attempt to move closer, but steadily maintained his distance. He returned the other man's smile and made a small gesture with his hand that Sir Kipp returned with a slight nod.

"I see that Desmond has taught you the lesson of humility."

Jaeme peered down at his armor and saw that the shirt of punishment jutted out through an armor joining. With a quick motion, he stuffed the bright cloth back and said, "It is a lesson I'll not soon forget."

Sir Kipp nodded. "Then here's another not to forget, my lord. Despite what you may feel about yourself, the men ride for you."

"What do you mean?" Jaeme asked, confused by the statement.

"All here know that you are not as experienced as they," the noble replied with a sweeping gesture toward the company at the rear. "You need not hide by distancing yourself from their company."

"You are not being fair, Kipp," Desmond interjected, finally pulling his horse closer. "Some of the knights harbor resentment that Jaeme is the new lord."

"Leave them to me and the others like me, who swear to support the Lord of Elfwood and not grouse about age and experience. Richard Mortimer was a man of character, and his son can be no less."

Sir Kipp slammed his visor back over his face and saluted to Jaeme again. Almost in a daze, the young lord saluted back, slowly lowering his hand as the knight rode back into the fog.

"It seems you have champions among the nobles," Laela

said. Like Jaeme, she was also a little stunned, but definitely pleased.

However, Desmond's silence made Jaeme realize something. "Which men do not feel I am fit to rule?" he asked the trainer pointedly.

Desmond turned his face away, his expression clearly showing that he had revealed something that was best left undiscovered for the moment. "There are some, like Bors and Gald, who believe that only the strong should rule. And if not the strong, then at least the old."

"What does age have to—?"

"An old ruler is a wise and strong ruler," the druidess said, interrupting Jaeme's question. To Desmond, she asked, "Will they cause trouble on the battlefield?"

The trainer shook his head in reply. "Not on the field. But afterward . . . who can say?"

The contingent of knights bivouacked in a small clearing that would have been within sight of Wycham Wood had the sun-devouring mists not blinded the eye worse than night. Jaeme discovered that it was sometimes difficult to find his way back to his place among the small fires kept burning for the men's comfort. Every once in a while he heard someone mention that a peasant's father, or perhaps daughter, had disappeared into the fog and never returned. He did not know what it could mean, or even if it were true.

The young lord felt somewhat out of place among the nobility, despite what the honest Sir Kipp had said. Jaeme was called "sir," but did not feel he had earned the title yet; the shirt of punishment was a constant reminder of just how much more he had to learn before he became a true knight. Though his training was mostly private, he had spent a great deal of time with the unlanded soldiers. He felt an affinity for them, and with them was often more comfortable.

Jaeme lifted his head, which he discovered was bent against the penetrating chill of the fog. He knew that he had to set an example for the men and nobles alike despite what he might feel about himself. Everyone must be prepared to engage the dragon, and from the battered appearance of Sir

Cedric's armor it was obvious that the fight would require courage, discipline, and a little bit of luck.

"A good day for a battle, eh, my lord?" a strong voice asked from Jaeme's left. Startled, the young lord turned and peered through the mists. The bearded noble sitting near the weak campfire flew the colors of the Fishers, but Jaeme could not quite place the knight's first name. He thought he recalled seeing the man at some court function, but everyone there had worn their family surcoats' not their field gear and helmets.

"A fine day indeed," Jaeme replied, voice equally potent. Hoping to raise some spirit of camaraderie, he added, "Are you prepared to engage a legendary foe?"

The noble laughed and said, "Prepared? What knight hasn't prayed for the day when he might vanquish a monster and save the land?"

"True enough!" another voice answered from around the fire. "We must be valiant this day, for another like it may not arise for a hundred years!"

More laughter erupted and echoed all around Jaeme, surrounding him with good cheer despite the inclement weather. He felt much better about the state of his troops as he added his own voice to the knights'. The laughter continued as he walked back to what he hoped was his place at the camp.

Jaeme's guess was correct. Laela and Desmond were still sitting where he had left them an hour before, whispering about something that the young lord could not quite make out. The druidess was dressed in her heaviest riding clothes, including a hooded cloak. Jaeme wondered if she no longer felt the cold as intensely as she had the first few nights of the fog, or if she just was more adept at hiding her discomfort. The question worried him more than the answer.

The thought of the young woman's chill made Jaeme think of the black caravan outside the walls of Castle Elfwood. He still had not heard anything about the wagons, either rumors from the farmers or information from his counselors, men-at-arms, or guards. The only thing definite was that the wagons seemed to evoke a fear equal to that created by the omnious clouds of choking fog.

"Jaeme!" Laela said happily when she saw the young

lord approach. "I thought you'd gotten lost." Standing, she noticed that he looked a little more cheerful than when he'd left.

Jaeme nodded and took the druidess's hand, guiding her back to the ground. "So did I," he replied, reaching out to pour himself a cup of tea from the kettle that hung above the flames on an iron tripod. He added with relief that flattered the druidess, "I did not think that I would ever find my way back."

"What did you discover?" Desmond inquired over the soft conversation. He drew his sword from its sheath, poured some of the kettle's water onto a whetting stone, and pulled the blade across it, producing a sound like that of screeching birds.

Wincing, the young lord said, "That what Sir Kipp said was true. And that the nobles have always dreamt of fighting a dragon."

"That's no surprise," Laela said, taking a sip of her own tea. She took no pleasure in the thought of battle for any reason.

Desmond nodded, but even in the fog, both Jaeme and Laela could see that his next comment was not one he found pleasant to repeat. "True enough. A knight lives for glory—"

"And what could be more glorious than a dragon?" Jaeme interjected.

"I've never put much stock in glory. For me, living well and ruling well are what's important, not the number of animal skins hanging on the walls."

Reaching under his cloak, Jaeme ran his finger over the punishment shirt. He realized now that Desmond had probably seen more battles and slaughter than any other person he knew. The trainer had taught combat skills to countless sons of nobles, and, more often than not, had seen the illusion of glory passed down through the years rather than the intelligence and wisdom necessary for a good baron or count. Though he had also reveled in the idea of victorious battles, Jaeme felt that through the guidance of his father he'd learned to ignore the potential spoils of war and instead look for other means to settle a conflict. He did not doubt that Desmond had something to do with the murdered lord's attitudes.

"Jaeme! Jaeme!"

The young lord turned just in time to be kicked in the stomach by a boy wearing the raiments of Castle Elfwood. The lad toppled over and nearly landed in the fire, but Desmond and Laela swiftly rose from their seats and pulled him away from the flames. He landed hard on his back but apparently was too excited to take notice of the burning fate from which he had just been saved.

The Lord of Elfwood saw that the boy was Skyler, his squire. "Jaeme!" Skyler cried again, gesturing wildly. "The scouts have come back! They've seen the dragon!"

With a final heave, Cedric dumped the remaining earth onto the grave site. Neither he nor Dec, who stood nearby, exhausted, recalled when they had started the burial. The old knight guessed that night would be falling within the hour.

The girl had finally gone to sleep after the magician had prevailed upon her to swallow a bit of herb mixed with sugar and water. Cedric was not pleased with the young man's sorcerous practices, either in this instance or when they were fleeing the villagers. However, he said nothing. He could contain his own distaste for the sake of others.

Wiping a heavy line of sweat off his brow, the huge knight speared his shovel into the ground, leaning on it for support. The air labored in his lungs though he knew that he was as strong as ever. Calluses from swordplay and horseback riding kept his hands from becoming furnaces of pain.

"Have you come up with any new ideas, Master Dec?" he asked. His voice was strong but a little hoarse.

The young magician did not stir for a moment, as his thoughts were on other matters. When he hadn't been busy digging, falling over, or peeling at blistering skin, he'd been trying to puzzle out exactly what had taken place inside the house and the sequence of events. He still felt that his initial conclusions had been correct; the parents obviously knew about the threat from outside and barricaded themselves from within. Their deaths may or may not have happened during dinner. They may have sat down to eat safe in the knowledge that they were suitably protected.

However, that still did not explain why the windows were left unbarred or what happened to the man and the woman. The food's temperature and the oil remaining in the lamp were no particular indicators of time, so it was difficult to tell when the parents had been killed.

"Have you come up with any new ideas?" Cedric inquired with more force.

Startled, Dec sat up and immediately saw stars flash before his eyes and heard the roar of the ocean in his ears. Around the strange taste of fish, he replied, "I was thinking about the bodies."

"It is evil work," the old knight said in a grim voice. "I've never seen its like before."

"And I've never *heard* of its like," Dec added. With a great groan, he struggled to his feet, leaning against a nearby tree for support. He let himself slip to the ground when his legs gave way again. His wound throbbed in time with his heart and the air would not enter his lungs free from the corruption of the fog. He realized there were times when the mists were so thick that Cedric vanished from sight.

Cedric left his shovel in the dirt and walked over to Dec, sitting down heavily. The magician was amazed that the knight, dressed in full armor, could labor so hard for so long.

"Don't be so surprised," Cedric said, peering into Dec's open face. "I've run miles in armor and then fought in battles that lasted a better part of the day."

"How do you do it?"

"Many factors. What you most likely haven't thought of is that, effectively, mail weighs less when you wear it."

The mage snapped his fingers in understanding. "Like a heavy cloak that feels like nothing."

"Like a cloak, aye," Cedric returned. "What did you discover about the husband and wife in your . . . studies?"

The obvious distaste in the old man's voice made Dec turn his face away and wince. Respect was what he desired, but he did not want that desire to make him feel ashamed for what he was, a mage. He supposed that one day he and the knight would have a lengthy discussion on morals and values.

What he had discovered, though, was very confusing to him, and would most likely be meaningless to Cedric. The old knight had said that he had never seen deaths like those of the man and woman, but Dec decided that the man's experience might provide some useful piece of information.

"I'm not really sure where to start," he replied, hedging.

"You opened up that little book of yours. Start with that."

Dec reached under his sweat-stained robes to pull out the book that contained a good number of his spells and the majority of his notes. His hand caught on a thread, and he felt bile rise to his mouth as the bandage across his shoulder shifted. He quickly freed himself and removed the tome. The book fell open to the page where he had most recently worked.

"Subjects were found dead on this date of our Lord, etcetera, etcetera," he began, thinking he sounded much like his father pouring over a legal document. However, he saw that Cedric obviously did not take well to an officious tone that spoke of people as nothing but "subjects." He quickly changed.

"The mother's and father's bones were crushed in accommodating the bodies to the shape of the chimney. There was little other damage to the bodies, leading us to believe that they were not tortured before they were killed."

Dec paused, staring into the fog. His notes seemed more objective than he felt. He was not sure if he could go on.

"Continue, Master Dec," Cedric said softly.

With a calming breath, Dec went on: "The similar expressions on their faces implies that lawful forces caused their deaths, while the cant of their eyes reflects cold and enervation—"

"I don't understand," the knight interrupted, piercing the mage with a sharp glance. "What do you mean, 'lawful forces,' and 'enervation'?"

"In my field of study, lawful forces are those that act in a lawful manner." Dec sought for the proper words. "A wave crashing against the shore is lawful, as is a fire burning wood."

"A wave in the ocean is never the same twice—"

"True, but the *motion* is the same, as is the effect," Dec replied. He hoped Cedric would not continue pursuing this line of questions.

The old knight rubbed his chin in thought. "Then what are non-lawful forces?"

"Non-lawful forces, what a mage would call *chaotic* forces, are those where the . . . for the sake of this argument, let me say that a chaotic force would be the ocean where the wave was born."

Before Cedric could proceed with another inquiry, Dec added, "The cant of the eye tells where life, or soul, escapes when it is removed. Enervation is the removal of energy from a body, in this case a person. Therefore," the mage concluded with a gesture toward the fresh graves, "their souls were taken to cold."

"And that means?"

Dec shrugged. His gaze lingered on the mound of dirt which was all that remained of a man and a woman, a husband and wife, father and mother. He wished that he could be with his parents, or just see their faces.

"I have to stop staring into the fog," the magician muttered, ending with a self-conscious laugh. Taking a deep breath, he added, "I don't know what it means, except that something, or somebody, stole their souls."

Cedric forced himself to ignore almost everything the young man had just stated. What Dec said was too fantastic to believe. Standing, the old knight brushed the dirt from his armor and ran his hands through his rough hair.

"I do not like the words you speak, Master Dec, nor do I understand or have the desire to understand them. We will take the girl with us when we leave for Castle Elfwood."

"I'll sit out here and think for a while," Dec called out as the knight plodded back to the little house. He was angry at Cedric's words, not because they were insulting, but because they implied a certain ignorance that desired to be perpetuated. To break the bounds of his own ignorance was one of the reasons Dec became a mage. However, he understood that Sir Cedric had no liking for magicians or their ways, and the man was old and wise enough to have good reasons.

Strangely, the thought of age brought back the faces of Jaeme and Laela. He wanted to send them a message, but felt that he should conserve his energies in case he needed to communicate with Albion about the dragon or this new mystery.

Dec suddenly became aware that somebody nearby was watching. He remembered the beautiful woman at the inn, the one who desired his life, and felt fear clutch at his heart. He quickly decided that the simplest spell of protection would be the best since it was the fastest.

"Good eve, my young friend," a man said, appearing out of the fog like an apparition.

"And good eve to you, sir," Dec returned. He had no intention of losing his advantage and kept his hands ready for the proper gesture.

If the man saw what the mage planned, he made no show of it. "May I speak with you a moment?"

"This is an odd place to meet," Dec said. He realized he was staring at the man's chest, which appeared to be bleeding from arrow wounds.

The man reached down and placed a hand on one of his wounds. He showed it stained with crimson to Dec with an odd combination of fear and sorrow on his face.

"Please excuse my state, but my time is short and we must speak."

"Who are you?" Dec asked, feeling isolated and hoping Cedric would come outside again. He was afraid that this man might be the one who destroyed the lives of the man and woman. He forgot to keep his hands in the proper positions for his spell.

"Do not fear, Decutonius Consulus. I am your friend. I am Richard Mortimer, Sixth Lord and Earl of Elfwood."

Chapter 9

THE LINES OF BATTLE WERE DRAWN UP IN A CLASSIC FASHION worked out by Sir Kipp. Jaeme was still lord and commander of the troops and his approval of any plan was final, but seeing the honorable knight's strategies was more than enough to convince him of the plan's efficacy.

Jaeme's hand was hard on the hilt of his father's sword. He had no intention of drawing it unless the battle became desperate, since he still did not know the nature of the weapon's magic. He kept a mundane broadsword in a sheath on his saddle as well as a lance which he kept propped against a stirrup.

He discovered that the nervousness he felt did not stem from concern for his own safety but for that of his troops and Laela. He no longer felt that the druidess should be in the line of battle and thought about asking her to return to the safety of the castle, or at least the baggage train behind. However, every time he turned to ask her go, she would engage him in some small point of conversation that led him away from his original intent.

Laela knew that Jaeme wanted her to leave, but she felt it

was her duty to both him and the Druidic Council to stay and at least witness the fight, if not become engaged in it. The safety of Elfwood depended on the knights' ability to quickly vanquish the beast before it could set too much of the forest aflame. Although she had no skill at combat, she figured she would at least be able to extinguish fires that threatened the wood.

Seeing the retinue of men and equipment gathered for this single task made the druidess angry that her own people were unwilling to contribute to the welfare of the land they were bound to protect. Despite the fact that they played at politics like any of the lords in this realm, she felt that the Council should have provided some additional assistance, a spell, or some magical weapon to fight the dragon. She vowed that if something happened to Jaeme because of the battle, she would personally see that the leaders of the druids were punished.

"Look ho!" one of the knights shouted, futilely waving his bannered lance in the hope that the other nobles would see him through the choking mists.

Jaeme's mount immediately stepped on something that cracked loudly, sounding like a broken log. Stopping, he bent down in the saddle and saw that there was a shattered lance buried deep in the soft earth. The banner on it was not familiar.

There were several other shouts from the knights and Jaeme answered the closest one.

"These are the banners of Penwarden's men," the noble muttered, dropping the little flag to the ground with obvious distaste.

"Why didn't they make an attempt to join forces with us?" Jaeme asked the knight. It was the same man he had talked with at the campfire. Jaeme was nervous now that he could actually see the results of a battle, and reminded himself that since this was his first he must be especially careful.

"For the glory, of course," the knight retorted. With a salute, he quickly galloped off to see what the others had found.

The idea that Penwarden desired the glory of killing the dragon himself, as well as the knight's obvious dislike for that lord, put everything into a new perspective for Jaeme. There was little doubt in his mind that if Albion and King Edmund heard about this great deed the riches and lands bestowed on Penwarden would be considerable. And with those new resources, there was a chance that Lord Penwarden might petition for war against Elfwood to gain its land as well.

"What's wrong, Jaeme?" Laela asked, noticing the young lord's clouded features.

Jaeme did not hear the druidess at first as his anger churned inside him. After a moment, he shook off the visions of possible feudal war and replied, "Nothing. Nothing at all. Let's ride."

Within fifteen minutes, Elfwood's force was at the edge of the forest. Riding close to Sir Kipp, Laela, and Desmond, and with Skyler at his side, Jaeme heard the knight order the archers to form a loose line and advance to the south of the clearing while the men-at-arms and knights on horseback made their way to the southeast. The young lord saw that this would allow the archers to fire at least two volleys over the heads of the nobles without danger of shooting their own troops.

"How many men do you suppose were in Penwarden's force?" Jaeme asked Sir Kipp as he looked over a fairly recent map of the wood.

Without glancing up, the man replied, "Around ten knights, perhaps a small unit of soldiers." Rolling the map back into a tube, he added, "Much less than ours."

"And our men are better trained, more valiant knights," Desmond interjected before Jaeme could ask another question. The young lord hoped that he did not seem too doubtful about the ability of his own forces.

"By far," Sir Kipp agreed.

Laela noticed that the last of the men-at-arms and archers had entered the wood. The fog was much thinner around the trees. She felt she should know why, but could not find an answer no matter how hard she tried.

"Laela, I want you to stay behind," Jaeme finally said. He had seen her peering into the wood and guessed that she was worried about his safety. He was worried about her as well.

"No, Jaeme, I'm coming with you," the druidess replied hotly. Now her attention was completely focused on staying with him during the battle and ensuring his well-being to the best of her ability.

Jaeme grew angry. In this matter, he knew he was correct and would not let himself be swayed. "Laela, I'm ordering you—"

"*Ordering*? Who do you think you are, ordering *me*?" Laela snapped. "I'm a representative of the Druidic Council, and as such—"

A huge gout of flame interrupted the argument, the heat bathing their faces in a warmth they had not felt since the fog appeared. Without another word, Jaeme spurred his horse, Firebrand, into a tight turn and bolted off through the wood, grabbing his lance out of the stirrup and hiking it beneath his armpit for better ease of motion. Instantly, Laela was on his heels, determined to see that he come to no harm.

The young lord maneuvered his steed through the woods so quickly that Laela doubted she could have followed even if she'd assumed the form of a rabbit. She was falling behind until Jaeme glanced back and slowed his pace so she could catch up. The anger she had previously felt seemed silly in light of the battle.

Jaeme saw that many of the archers were fleeing and yelling in fear. He would have tried to rally them if not for the fact that none of the knights had yet to appear. Another stream of flame lit the depths of the woods, and the young lord barely made out the line of horsemen against the titantic shadow of the legendary beast. The sight made him ride faster.

He made the boundary of the wood within moments and discovered that the knights made continuing charges against the dragon, driving their proud lances against the monster's scaled hide with little effect. The few remaining men-at-arms formed small lines of protection against the beast's rending claws, dragging off fallen riders and recovering horses. Jaeme saw that only a handful of the knights were still mounted and that the rest were injured from falls or missing.

The dragon's wings buffeted the air, sending up a cloud of dust that made Jaeme's eyes sting and forced him to gasp for air. Though his frightened horse tried to bolt, he skillfully maintained its stance. Laela was nowhere to be found, and that wrenched Jaeme's heart with a fear equal to none he had ever encountered.

But his loyal soldiers required his aid, and he would do all he could against the monster. Bringing his lance up to the level of the dragon's swaying stomach, Jaeme lowered the visor of his helm and settled himself into the saddle. He heard Desmond's voice telling him to always watch the tip of the lance, and the deep well of his father's voice telling him to find bravery. The dragon's huge black body stepped out of the maelstrom it had created, giving the young lord a full view of its terrifying aspect—red eyes, scales thicker than plate, claws sharper than the sharpest sword. . . .

Jaeme closed the distance to the black beast within the span of a heartbeat. He felt the lance contact the scales of the monster's hide at the stomach, felt the hope that his weapon had struck true to its mark. The shaft of the lance shattered, and Firebrand continued its charge around one of the legs of the dragon. Jaeme saw that he was falling from his mount and could do nothing to save himself as the horse made a mighty leap over the dragon's thrashing tail.

Hitting the ground made Jaeme's shoulder go numb, and he would have pulled his father's sword but he could not feel his hand. To his terror, the dragon's sharp serpentine head turned and he was transfixed by the baleful red glare of its eyes for what seemed a lifetime. He willed his arm to slowly draw the magicked blade and his legs to maneuver him away from the gigantic claw which threatened to tear him apart—

For a moment, Jaeme thought he saw a hawk appear in the air before him. He was suddenly knocked out of the way of the claw by the body of Laela, who grappled with him and forced him to the ground. The dragon's talons dredged the earth where the two had just stood.

"We've got to move!" the druidess yelled over the roar of flame that was burning the ground in the clearing. Worried about the welfare of his men, Jaeme held back, resisting.

"What about—?"

"Everyone's gone, Jaeme! They're all retreating to Elfwood!"

"I suppose you wouldn't mind if I decided that for myself?" Dec asked petulantly. Still seated, he edged away from the ghostly presence until his back pressed up against a tree. His hand came up, and his fingers began casting his protection cantrip.

"I said you have naught to fear!" the apparition vociferated, pointing a commanding finger at the young mage. Dec's hands dropped into his lap. The fear he felt was not supernatural; it stemmed from a voice of power that was accustomed to having orders heeded.

The magician swallowed hard, hoping that Cedric might have heard the ghost's shout and come running to the rescue. Unfortunately, that did not seem to be the case. "What do you want?"

Lowering its hand with an expression that Dec thought to be a strange mixture of relief and embarrassment, the spirit sought about in the fog for a place to sit. After a moment, it sighed and sat on the ground, lifting its blood-soaked surcoat from underneath.

"We have never met, but I know that you are acquainted with my son," the apparition stated calmly.

"Who is your son?"

"Jaeme, of course."

Dec stared off into the fog and gathered his thoughts. He realized that Jaeme's last name was Mortimer. He also remembered something about the lies of the spirit world. The apparition's face was as open as the mage could expect and held the same handsome lines as the new Lord of Elfwood.

"Your son grieves for your life," Dec said. Jaeme's pain was obvious to the mage from his first days at the castle. Dec wanted to make up for his precipitant abandoning of the keep by telling Jaeme's father everything he could recall about the new lord. "He has not found your murderers."

Richard Mortimer lowered his head and peered down into his chest. He ran his hand over the horrible wounds and shuddered, as if in mortal agony; his fingers came back as bloody as the setting sun. Dec saw that the ghost's face remained calm.

"Neither have I," Richard Mortimer whispered. He lifted his head and smiled reassuringly at the mage, putting his hands in his lap. "I could have been a vengeful spirit, one of the many in this world, but decided against it. There are too many items this day that need to come to light."

"You were never known as a vengeful man," Dec said. "But as for things coming to light, this damned fog makes it seem the land will never see the sun."

Dec felt he could respect this spirit as much as he respected the living presence of Sir Cedric. Being candid was part of that respect.

"And if it has its way, mortal eyes *will* never see light again." Fearful, Dec made to speak, but the ghost of Richard Mortimer raised his hand for silence. "Decutonius Consulus, what I am about to say to you must reach the ears of my living son before three days pass. My murder was only the beginning of a plan to destroy Elfwood and thereby the magic that is the life of the world.

"My killers knew nothing of this plan, thinking their part in it was only to capture the lands of my keep. They were manipulated into weakening the defenses of Elfwood Forest."

"Through your death," Dec added rhetorically. He thought he was beginning to understand something of what the spirit was saying.

The apparition nodded confirmation. "I could not perform my sacred duty as guardian of the forest. There was not time enough to tell Jaeme."

"So what you are saying is that there is a connection

between the forest and what keeps the world—alive?'' the young mage ventured. He was no longer sure he understood what was being discussed.

''You are correct. It is the charge of the Lords of Elfwood to defend the forest, and thereby, the world,'' Richard Mortimore replied.

''And the dragon is this evil?''

The spirit appeared confused. ''I know of no dragon.''

The answer stunned and confused Dec. Though he had never been convinced that the dragon was the one causing the fog, he had no other information with which to formulate a theory. Though this eliminated one explanation, it did not leave enough facts to postulate another.

Another piece of information suddenly materialized in the mage's thoughts. ''Why can't you just tell me everything you are trying to say?''

''I cannot tell you directly what I am trying to say,'' the ghost answered. Its voice was filled with regret and Dec was sorry he had asked the question. The reply meant that there was some kind of law that the spirit must obey that did not allow it to come out and say everything that was on its mind. Apparently, it *could* answer questions.

''All right,'' the mage began, leaning forward from his haven against the tree. ''You were killed by unknown assailants who were being manipulated without their knowledge into weakening the defense of Elfwood Forest. This means that there is another force at work that has brought this accursed fog and cold to the land. And it's not the dragon,'' he added.

''Not the dragon,'' Mortimer agreed.

The spirit suddenly cocked its head as if listening in fear. Its hands went to the bleeding wounds in its chest.

Dec listened for a moment. He heard nothing but didn't question the ghost, figuring it wouldn't be able to describe what it heard. Additionally, he noticed that the ghost's replies had become much shorter. He went on with his inferences, hoping to take the apparition's mind off its fear. ''This other force wants to destroy the Elfwood and thereby the world. It must have something to gain.''

"Of course."

"We found the parents of a young girl dead in that house," the magician stated, pointing back to the little home with the oil lamp still lit in the window. "Their spirits were taken to cold. This fog is cold. Therefore their deaths are related to whatever is causing this fog."

Dec waited for a reply. It seemed that the spirit of Richard Mortimer no longer listened to the young mage's words but to some unseen host in the ramparts of mist. Fearing time was short, Dec hastily continued.

"The fact that the windows were unbarred but the door was barricaded implies that this force could only enter through a normal entrance. . . ." Dec's voice trailed off a moment, but then he snapped his fingers and let himself follow his own trail of logic. "And that means that this force, obviously magical, requires some kind of permission to enter a home; otherwise it *would* have come through the windows."

The mage remembered legends of creatures that could come into someone's house only if allowed by the owner, but they were rare, and the creatures powerful. Peering into the ghost's gaunt and pain-filled face, Dec hoped to find some confirmation, but Mortimer didn't answer; he only listened.

"The doors were still barricaded, so the force did not enter there. The windows were closed. The only place left was . . . the chimney," the mage concluded, his throat going tight. The heavy mists had finally soaked him all the way through to his undergarments, and he felt unusually vulnerable, sitting in the haze talking with the dead lord, who now stood pensively. But Dec's mind was working with a speed that was familiar and made him more comfortable. He forced all his other feelings to the back of his mind.

"The parents must have needed a reason to give permission. The girl was outside and they were threatening her, so the mother and father gave in. They brought the girl in through the chimney, for what I can only assume was part of some malicious game, then killed the parents, leaving everything behind untouched.''

Dec shook his head. He felt that he could cry. He realized that he had called the force ''they,'' without thinking. Intuitively, he knew this was a correct term; in his mind, there must have been more than one in this ''force.'' And they were cruel and uncaring and tortured little girls with the horror of dead parents.

''You understand much, Decutonius,'' the spirit muttered absently. The mage saw that Richard Mortimer's shoulders were slumped like a man about to receive a beating. Dec did not think this was proper for a lord of such obvious stature.

''What can I do to help?'' he asked, drawing nearer the apparition.

''You know all you must know. Seek out my son, or in three days—''

Dec found himself, without warning, standing alone in the middle of the fog. He began to shiver from the penetrating cold and the idea that he was actually alone in the unnatural dark.

Before he left for the relative comfort of the house where Cedric waited with the little girl, Dec prodded the ground where Richard had stood. He picked something up off the ground and saw it was a piece of a signet ring with the heraldry of Elfwood. The metal was in good condition but the lacquer of the crest was shattered.

Pocketing the keepsake, Dec quickly walked back to the house. He realized that, in the end, he had finally thought of the spirit as a man.

Chapter 10

JAEME STARED INTO THE BLADE OF THE MAGIC SWORD AND SAW HIS own eyes stare back at him—black, piercing eyes, as sharp as the blade. He felt something on his shoulders, something heavy and familiar and sorely missed. The scent of his father entered his nostrils.

"Is there something amiss, m'lord?" Sejanus inquired, stepped forward in concern.

Blinking, the young lord quickly cleared his thoughts and brought his mind back to the matter at hand. "No, nothing. I'm sorry, what were you saying, Sejanus?"

"Merely that perhaps Lord Penwarden could now be asked for assistance," the advisor replied.

"And how do you suggest we approach him?" Counselor Teves asked incredulously. "What with his force already gone."

"There is no proof of that. Not a body was found," Sejanus countered, narrowing his eyes in anger.

Before Jaeme could intervene in the bickering, the last counselor said, "And what do you think the chances are that they've been eaten by the monster, Sejanus? The armor and weapons found were obviously masticated!''

''Gentlemen, please!'' Jaeme finally said, insinuating himself in the group of three advisors at the foot of the throne. He put his hands on his hips and sighed before continuing. ''This does not help our situation. The fog makes it impossible for any ship to leave or find the coast, and our court magician is missing—''

''Grave matters, indeed,'' Counselor Sejanus whispered reverently under his breath.

''—and I need all the options I can find. I will send Joseph as emissary from Elfwood to seek Penwarden's aid. Now, what else can you offer me?''

It was a long time before any of the old advisors spoke, and when they did, it was only to mumble incomprehensibly. Teves mentioned the name of Felker, then went no further when he saw the old hatred blaze up in Jaeme's eyes. Jaeme had not thought of Felker, in light of recent events, and did not want to be reminded of the man he suspected of murdering his father.

The young lord sat back down heavily on the uncomfortable throne. He guessed that if the chair had been easier to sit in, he might have been willing to wait until the late hours of the night for an answer, but as it was, he was unwilling to wait another minute.

''Very well,'' he began, gesturing with the silver-sheathed sword. He was unsure where this line of conversation was leading, but he followed it anyway. ''We are effectively stuck here until we get word from Penwarden.''

''But what if—'' Teves began, stepping forward.

Jaeme held up the sword for silence. ''Whether or not he cooperates, Elfwood and its lands must be prepared for the worst. Send word to the people of the realm that they are to remain within—a few hundred paces of their homes, for safety,'' he said, almost using the word ''sight.'' The choking fog made it obvious that there was little use for sight.

''If the dragon is discovered, they are to report immediately back to the keep. If there are no further questions, I would ask to be alone.''

The advisors stood perfectly still and Jaeme thought they were going to call him mad and demand he relinquish his right to the throne. However, he saw that Leker and Teves appeared pleased with the edict. Sejanus obviously expected something a bit more spectacular.

Laela passed the three men on her way into the Great Hall and saw that two of the three seemed mildly happy with something. She wished that she had been told of this meeting.

''I'm sorry, Laela, but you were still asleep and—''

''It's all right, Jaeme. When was the last time *you* slept?''

The young lord felt the burdens of his office weigh upon his shoulders like never before. For some reason, a vision of the black caravan outside the castle walls came to his mind. The wagons had not moved since the day they'd arrived, and none of the guards had seen a single soul leave. Fear of what might lurk in the strange fog prevented anyone from approaching the mysterious wagon train for further investigation. He had felt some fear himself when he returned with the wounded from the fight with the dragon.

Jaeme lay the sheathed blade carefully across his knees and rubbed his face with his hands. In fact, he *couldn't* remember the last time he had rested.

Laela stepped near the throne, reached out a tentative hand and then drew it back, changing her mind. She did not want Jaeme to be thinking about anything more than he had to, no matter her own growing feelings on the matter. ''As your advisor, I suggest you get some sleep immediately.''

''And as my friend?''

The druidess's heart leapt at the sound of the last word, deep, hungry, and perhaps pleading. She did not answer immediately, unsure if everything she'd read into the statement was actually so.

''As your friend, I'm *telling* you to go to bed.''

Of all the things flowing through the river of Jaeme's thoughts at the moment, Laela was the most prominent, though it seemed that his father was somewhere nearby, dead but close enough to touch. Jaeme recalled the times that he and the red-haired woman had been together and the times that he had stopped himself from touching her, fighting the longing. And now, though he wanted to hold her more than ever, he was too tired and, strangely, too rational to allow himself the luxury of her wished-for company.

"How are the wounded faring?" he inquired, pushing everything from his mind.

Pursing her lips in concern and disappointment, Laela replied, "They are fine. Through some miracle, the dragon did not kill a single man. There must have been a guardian spirit nearby."

"That is the only good news I have heard in quite some time," the young lord whispered, continuing to rub his face. The idea of sleep was enticing.

"What did the counselors say?"

"Nothing worth repeating. I issued a decree ordering the townspeople and farmers to stay within a reasonable distance of their homes. What else can I do?"

The urge to console Jaeme overwhelmed the druidess, and she stepped up to the throne and put her hands on the young lord's shoulders. Jaeme immediately tensed, pleased but startled by the sudden display of affection. Laela felt his muscles twist into knots. She almost pulled back but knew that if she released him now, she'd never be able to look into those dark eyes again.

Jaeme let himself relax. Though Laela's touch was all he truly craved at times, he reminded himself that he was still responsible for the lives of hundreds of people. He would do nothing more than accept her comfort.

"That feels . . . nice," he murmured. He told himself that he could still take some pleasure.

"Have you thought about hiring mercenaries?" Laela asked, feeling her hands grow warm with every kneading grasp.

"'Mercenaries are expensive and unreliable at best,'" Jaeme quoted, letting his head fall forward. The druidess moved from the young lord's shoulders to his neck, then back again when she felt her work done for the moment.

"Who said that?"

Jaeme's hands gripped the sheathed blade, pressing the weapon against his flesh so hard he could feel his bones grind. "My father, in a lecture to me about being a lord. The other nobles have said as much."

Laela continued kneading, making her way down to the small of Jaeme's back, then returning to his shoulders, leaning close against his body. To her sensitive nose, he smelled of fear, anguish, and pain, but mostly fear.

"What if I were to ask the Druidic Council for help?" she asked on inspiration. Her hands were very tired.

The young lord spun in his chair and grabbed the druidess by the wrists. His eyes blazed and she thought she might fall into them if she allowed herself.

"No! I won't let you leave the castle!"

"Haven't we talked about this before? I told you not to give me orders," Laela said in a tone that was neither sharp nor barbed. She felt no desire to argue.

Jaeme, however, was not finished. "The dragon is at large, eating and destroying! Who knows what it might do to you if it found you!"

"But you said—"

"Never mind what I said! The fact is there is no way I'm going to allow you to risk your life. I don't know what I'd do if you were . . ."

The young lord was about to say "killed," but changed his mind. "Gone," he said instead.

"Thank you, Jaeme. But times call for strict measures. I am up to the task. I am a druidess from the Council of Elfwood," Laela declared firmly. "I am capable of taking care of myself."

Jaeme released her wrists. In his mind, he knew she was right. In his heart, there was nothing more wrong in the world. He felt defeated.

"How long will it take you to return?" he asked leadenly.

"No more than a day. I'll take the form of a hawk."

"Very well, then, Laela. I cannot order you to stay, and

what you propose could be of great benefit to the citizens of the realm. But you will be sorely missed,'' the young lord added.

Laela nodded, tucking her hands inside her heavy robes. She bowed once and turned to leave.

''I'll be back, Jaeme, and with help.''

''I know. Return soon.''

''What is happening?'' Laela demanded. She was almost reeling with grief.

The walls of the Druidic Council Hall were grey and desiccated, the venerable trees that once formed the living archways nearly dead. Brittle leaves littered the floor and blackened Laela's bare feet. The cold fog rolled in like small clouds.

The three druidic elders, seemingly as lifeless as the Hall, regarded her with plaintive eyes. ''We do not know . . .'' one said, his face covered with blue dye.

''We die . . .'' the second added.

The last, who Laela knew to be the oldest of the three, attempted to speak but obviously could not find the strength.

''When did this start?'' the druidess demanded. ''Why didn't you tell me?'' Hot tears filled her eyes and created patches on her cheeks where the airborne dust of the woods had dirtied them.

The first elder replied, ''When the fog came, we all felt unbearably cold . . .''

''Some died . . .''

Again, the oldest druid attempted to speak but did not find the strength. He put his face down into his arms and lay on the table like a child overcome by sleep. Laela saw that his shoulders jerked with slight sobs.

Nearly overcome by a depresson that she'd heard had often engulfed the hearts of those in Castle Elfwood when they stared into the roiling mists, Laela sat heavily on the floor. She waved her hands in front of her face to disperse the swarm of dust motes that danced before her eyes. Sitting in the presence of the elders would normally be unthinkable, but at the moment courtesy and tradition were the least of her concerns.

"I also felt this cold," Laela said, remembering the shivering that had overcome her. "But it stopped after a while."

"Here, it does not stop. Here, it becomes worse," the second elder said.

"We do not know whence it comes," the first elder interjected before the druidess could voice her next question. "It comes from everywhere, not from the points on the compass."

Laela nodded in reply, rubbing her eyes to remove the dust in them. Unfortunately, the dust on her hands added to that in her eyes and she was forced to use an equally dirty sleeve to aid herself. Blinking hard, she asked, "Was there no way to stop it?"

The first elder shook his head, but the second elder answered, saying, "The mists penetrated even the thickest wood and no spell we had could keep it from entering our free homes."

Sighing, the young druidess imagined how the rest of the forest must appear. The trees she climbed were most likely wet with rot, the fields dark and damp, and the streams too cold in which to play. Her own home had been dark, defiled by the fog.

Laela stood firmly and brushed herself off. Steeling herself against the grief of the three broken men who stood before her, she stated, "There is a danger to the Elfwood that has not been defeated. The dragon continues to lounge in Wycham Wood unchecked."

The oldest druid raised his head for a moment, then slumped back into his depression. His shoulders continued to heave.

Ignoring the sight as best she could, Laela continued: "The men of Castle Elfwood have not been able to defeat the serpent, and the court magician is missing. The Druidic Council must do something to help."

Laela waited for an answer. She was met with nothing but stony, depressing silence. There was no wind to howl through the maze of the druids' wood, and the fog seemed to moan and roil and rejoice in its victory. She did not know the source of the mists, but if the dragon was the cause, Laela was determined to have it vanquished.

"What help can you afford?" she asked more bluntly. No matter what their condition, the druidess was not going to let the Council die from despair. She felt a strength within herself that they apparently could not find in their own hearts.

"What would you ask of us?" the first druid inquired weakly.

"We have nothing to give," intoned the second.

"We have the Charming."

Laela stepped back in surprise as the third and oldest high druid lifted himself up out of his depression to face her. His face was older and held more lines than she last remembered, when the Council had sent her as envoy to Castle Elfwood, but his eyes were still bright. "We have the Charming," the old man repeated.

The other two druids blinked rapidly, as if waking from a dream. They looked to each other, and Laela thought she saw the first man almost smile.

"What is the Charming?"

The oldest druid half-rose from his seat. He kept himself up by leaning on the table. He said, "The Charming is not a spell, not an incantation."

"It is a form of . . . influence," the first druid added.

The second elder nodded in confirmation. "Influence upon those whose true name you know."

For a moment, Laela had been elated, but now she was confused. "What do you mean?" she asked. "What is a 'true name'?"

The three druids turned their backs to Laela, leaving her even more perplexed. They appeared to be conferring about something and their words were too hushed to hear. The druidess did her best to keep herself from becoming nervous or angry and found herself thinking of Jaeme, and, strangely, Sir Cedric.

Finally, the elders turned back to face her. "We have

decided that you should know the meaning of the true name,'' the first said.

The second shifted uncomfortably, and Laela thought that he was not altogether pleased with the decision, though his red-dyed face showed nothing in the dim light. However, he said, ''All things were given a true name at the time of Creation.''

''And those that know the true name of a person can force compulsion,'' the first druid added.

Laela started to shrug in confusion, but she stopped herself, out of respect for the Council and also to bolster their burgeoning hope. ''The dragon is not a person, nor do I know its 'true name,' '' she replied.

''The Charming also works on greater creatures like dragons,'' the second elder said, waving a triumphant finger in the air. He started to cough violently, and the expression of happiness that flitted across his face vanished in his pain.

The first druid helped his fellow councilor while saying, ''And though we do not know the name of the dragon, we know the true name of dragonkind.''

The third elder stood feebly, laboring his way through the fog in such a way that Laela thought the mists pushed physically against the man's advance. The druid stood before her and held out a small scroll made from wide leaves.

''Within this document you will find the true name of dragons. We must have your oath, Laelestequenstrutia, that you will use this power with prudence and without thought to furthering your own desires.''

Laela slowly reached out for the scroll, unsure of what the man could mean by his last statement. The wide leaves were still fresh and green, holding some small amount of moisture. The druidess held onto the scroll as if it were the last piece of life in the forest that was her true home. In her hand there was enough power to sway the lives of thousands, slay any enemy, perhaps control all of Albion. The might of dragons was said to be immense and terrible, and she could do what she wished—

Suddenly, Laela dropped the scroll to the floor as if it

burned her hand. She backed away from it in fear, her heart beating so fast she felt as if she had transformed herself into a rabbit and run for hundreds of miles. She did not want to touch the leaves: they contained too much power. Though she did not fully understand the use of the naming cantrip, the druidess felt that the chance for mischief and abuse was great enough that it should never be used.

"You are wise, Laelestequenstrutia. We entrust you with the true name of dragons," the third elder said.

Laela felt, rather than thought, a name crawl through her mind. It was a scaly name, long and powerful, which breathed flame, acid, cold. The name flew and slept for hundreds of years and awoke only when hungry. It boasted a history older than Albion, Elfwood Forest, or the mountains. It was the true name of dragonkind, and Laela understood how the creatures might be coerced.

"Leave, return to your Jaeme," the third elder commanded, though his voice was like dust in the wind. "Go now and save your home."

Despite the fact that she wanted desperately to return to Castle Elfwood, Laela made a single stop before she left.

Myrna sat in a chair in her simple home, appearing much older than when the young druidess had last visited. As elsewhere in the forest, the accursed mists curled through the elderly woman's house. The cold dampened the once-familiar smells of flowers and herbs.

"Laela!" Myrna exclaimed, slowly standing. "Lewtt has been asking about you."

The young druidess hugged her mentor and adopted mother, and tried not to let her face show that she felt the despair within the old woman's heart.

"How is he?" Laela asked.

"Very well, or as well as the cold allows," Myrna said. "How fare you among men?"

"As well as can be expected," Laela whispered. She was glad to hear that Lewtt, her wood sprite friend, was in good health. Since the fighting at Castle Elfwood against Talvice the mercenary, Laela had felt it best to leave the wood sprite behind in the forest where he would be most comfortable.

"As I thought," Myrna replied, wagging her finger. She returned to her chair and gestured for Laela to be seated.

The greenwood chair that Laela had once thought so inviting was now brittle and hard, but she did not make a show of her discomfort. "I have met many—interesting, people."

"Really?" Myrna said. She picked up a hardened pine-needle, threaded it with a discarded animal hair, and tried to mend the dress she wore. Her hands shook.

"The cold," she murmured apologetically, putting the needle back on the table and rubbing her fingers for warmth.

"Why don't I still feel the chill?"

Myrna smiled. "You have something to give you warmth."

The young druidess nodded self-consciously; Myrna obviously meant Jaeme. Ignoring the statement as best she could for modesty's sake, Laela got up from the unpleasant chair and bent down to help her surrogate mother. "Yes, I have met many interesting people. And my duties keep me very busy."

"How do you like the new Lord of Elfwood now?"

Laela made a few stitches near the hem of Myrna's skirt and said, "Jaeme? He's quite the gentleman. Not at all what I originally expected."

"And the wizard?"

"Dec is something to be reckoned with."

"Oh, yes," Myrna replied, laughing a little. "I heard that the Great Elder had words with him."

The young druidess nodded and smiled. "Very true. I don't know what was said, but the effect was considerable."

"You'd be surprised at the effect of some words."

"Then you know of the Charming," Laela replied, looking up. For the first time she wondered why the elders did not use the Charming themselves. She guessed that it might have something to do with politics, or perhaps they could not use any magic because of their stultifying depression.

Myrna raised her eyes in surprise. ''I know of the the Charming, yes, but I was just thinking of something else.''

''What?''

''It's not important . . .''

Laela pulled on the hem several times like a little girl, and smiled playfully. ''Tell me,'' she implored.

''I was just thinking of a man your mother once knew. Tall and handsome. And proud,'' she added, her face darkening slightly.

''What happened?''

Myrna sighed in what Laela thought was discontent. ''He did not like the ways of magic and so left your mother despite their love.''

Something in both the words and the way they were spoken made Laela think back to a recent time at Castle Elfwood, but she couldn't quite recall what event it was that caused her to react to the statement. Peering up into Myrna's face, which appeared gaunt and unhappy in the thin fog that permeated the room, she inquired, ''What was the name of this man?''

''I can't seem to remember, though he did have dark eyes and a powerful voice,'' the old druidess replied. ''I think he was a knight, or going to be.''

Snapping the thread from the skirt, Laela stood up and placed the sewing tools back on the table. She glanced about the room and saw all the old accouterments of her childhood—bottles, pouches, the ceiling filled with knots, and the floor smooth as calm water. She had taken most of these things for granted, and only now did she realize that the house itself had a history older than her memory.

She sighed heavily. Though she did not understand the significance, in her heart she knew that the man of whom Myrna spoke could only be Sir Cedric of Penwarden.

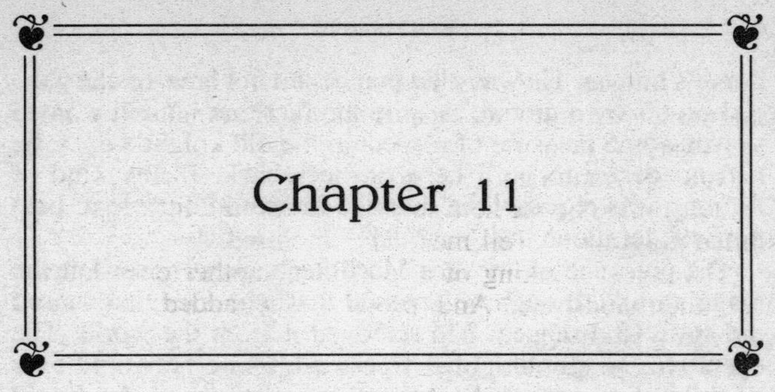

Chapter 11

Dec, Cedric, and the little girl left the dead parents' home as they had found it. The lamp, which the young mage noticed never seemed to run out of oil, continued to burn with a mournful light in the window.

Dec had given the girl another dose of the sugared potion to help her sleep, and this time she drank it without urging. Cedric had watched her willingly take the cup, thinking that perhaps she wished to go wherever her dreams would take her and escape the horrors of the real world. As the little house finally disappeared into the fog, he decided that to forget this place might be best.

Rowene, which was the child's name, rode draped over the saddle of Cedric's horse. Considering the dangers they had encountered, Cedric might better have put Rowene on the magician's horse, giving himself more maneuverability. He decided, however, that Dec's lack of riding experience would only cause greater harm if they all needed to escape. Cedric would do his best if there was fighting.

The mists continued to coil around the forest, and Dec found it nearly impossible to see the road beneath his horse's hooves. He was glad that he did not have to carry the girl on his own mount; despite the fact that he still wanted to gain some measure of respect in the old knight's eyes, he had no desire to be a hero on horseback. If any kind of fighting was required, he doubted he would be able to help himself, let alone another rider.

The presence of Richard Mortimer's ghost never left the mage's mind, though he guessed that whatever had caused the spirit to disappear had removed it from the world. The event was so stunning that Dec wasn't sure he would ever be rid of the memory; he was not sure if he wanted to be rid of it. He had met a man legendary in both deed and honor, the father of his new friend and lord, and the holder of a trust that extended back through the entire family line of Elfwood.

What troubled him was the way to broach the subject to Cedric. The knight appeared to be in no mood for conversation, and though Dec felt the man would be tolerant, he was not sure of his own credibility, especially after the incident at the inn with the woman in his dream.

"Or was it a dream?" he asked himself softly, attempting to remember. He stared out into the grey of the mists and felt that the fog gave all memory a certain solidity, a concreteness that was frightening.

"What did you say?" Cedric inquired without turning back from his place high atop Pele. The huge war horse continued to plod without question or complaint through the ramparts of moist air.

Dec felt that the opportunity had come to divulge his secret. He pondered a few moments on what to say, but he could come up with nothing. If he were going to tell his father about some new prank that had cost the Magisterium Lundinium a roof and several instructors, he would simply make up a fabulous excuse about what went wrong. He knew that Cedric was not a man that was going to listen to obvious lies or hedging.

In his heart, he had the answer, though it was hard to implement. He mumbled something under his breath.

"What? What did you say?"

The mage cringed. Cedric's words were harsh, unforgiving, and he was clearly not in the mood for idle talk. Dec thought for a moment about the hardships that the elderly man must have gone through in his life, only to be riding in a fog-clouded wood with an unconscious child and prattling magician. He felt somewhat ashamed of himself for not having the candor the old knight deserved.

"I saw a ghost last night," Dec said strongly.

He waited for the knight's answer, and his tension began to rise when there was no reply. Then, Cedric spoke. His voice was soft. "I, too, saw a ghost last eve."

The mage was stunned. "Really? Where? Was it the same one—"

"I saw a ghost last night as I stared out into the fog with Rowene finally asleep in my lap," the old knight interrupted, apparently lost in his own thoughts and ignoring what Dec had to say. "It was a woman, and her appearance was familiar, red hair and green eyes. . . ."

"Sounds like Laela," Dec muttered dejectedly. He had expected to be questioned, or even berated for coming up with wild stories, but being ignored was an option he had never considered.

Cedric stopped Pele in midstep and turned the horse so that he might face the magician. Dec stopped his horse in turn, pulling so hard on the rein in fear of some kind of retaliation that the animal walked backwards a few steps.

"You are exactly right," the old knight replied, sounding bewildered. Cedric's thoughts raced from Laela to the memory of a woman he had thought he saw in the young druidess's face, a woman he had loved and left so many years ago. Now he was alone and could not bear the thought that his family line would end with him.

"I said I saw a ghost last night," Dec repeated bravely. The old knight's behavior was so confusing that most of the mage's fear flaked away. All he wanted was a reply, no matter what the consequence.

Cedric lifted his face, and his dark eyes were like pools of night beneath his open visor. Dec shrank in his saddle, and he noticed that even his horse backed away from the old knight's dreadful countenance. "You saw *what* in the night?"

"Ghost—a ghost."

"And who was this tortured spirit?" Cedric inquired, his voice strong and loud. He was less than eager to hear another of the mage's stories of nocturnal visitors.

Dec plunged ahead violently. "It was Jaeme's father, Richard Mortimer."

"Do not speak so of the lord's sire!" Cedric commanded. Pele had leapt near Dec's mount faster than the mage could remember witnessing. The knight was a vision of fury and righteousness; Dec wondered how any foe could stand up to Cedric's might. Only his desire to be respected kept the magician from being intimidated. Without another word, he reached under his cloak and removed the piece of signet ring that he had discovered lying on the ground.

Cedric, angry at first, realized that the young man believed that he *had* seen Richard Mortimer's spirit. Regretting his hasty words, he reached out with a gauntleted hand to take the shattered lacquer emblem. He forced his features to soften as he examined the curiosity.

"It is part of a signet ring," he said.

Dec slowly released the breath that he had been holding so tightly within his chest. "Yes, and with the heraldry of Elfwood," he replied, glad that Cedric no longer seemed to be angry.

The old knight was skeptical, but he was careful not to let it show on his face. "How can you be sure? This area could have once been the kingdom of a number of past lords."

"I am sure because Richard Mortimer spoke to me last night. This is from his ring," the mage declared, pointing into the knight's armored palm.

Cedric did not wish to argue with the boy, but felt that there had been no ghost. However, to keep the mage happy, he decided to go along with Dec's story. "What did this spirit say to you?" he inquired evenly.

"That he had been murdered in these woods, and that there was a great evil on the land." Dec ignored Cedric's use of the word "this," which implied that the knight was not wholly convinced.

"At least half of that is obvious," Cedric said, rolling the lacquered chunk around in his palm. He remembered the ring of his sire, which he kept under at his waist when he wore his mail, and felt a touch of melancholy. "Did it say anything more specific?"

Dec wanted to tell him of the magic that was Elfwood infusing the rest of the world with life, but he doubted that Cedric would understand, or care to understand, the words. The ghost had ordered that Jaeme be told of the duty of the lords of Elfwood to protect the forest, but again that was an item the old knight would rather not hear. There were, however, two things that related directly to their immediate situation which he felt might sway the noble's opinion.

"Specifically, Richard Mortimer said that the girl's parents were killed by the those that created the fog, and that the dragon is not the cause!"

"What? What is this you are—"

Both men suddenly turned at the sound of running coming up from behind them, and both saw the angry flare of torches toiling through the curling mists.

"The peasants!" Dec hissed, crouching low on his horse. "What are we—"

Cedric grabbed the reins from the mage's tight grip and whispered, "We must leave if we are to save Rowene's life!" He began to guide the horses further up the road, but Dec saw that there were other torches to the right and to the left. With a gesture, he pointed out the advancing townspeople. He felt his heart pound in his chest and wondered how Cedric could always take everything with such aplomb.

The old knight weighed his options grimly. He saw that they were about to be surrounded by a mob that was undoubtedly bent on killing them. He had to save Dec's life and the life of the girl. He had to raise an army to fight the dragon and rid the land of its greatest peril. To do these things, he would have to live.

Cedric quietly drew his sword from its well-oiled sheath. He quickly formulated a plan that would allow him to cut through the pursuing mob, which had now circled around them and were closing like a noose.

A huge gout of flame erupted far across the land, startling Jaeme from his place by the window where he had moved the throne. He threw his arms up to protect his face, then dropped them to his lap with an expression of self-deprecation, hands falling to the warmth of the silver blade lying across his knees. He told himself that the flames must be on the other side of the wood, near Wycham. He thought he still felt the heat.

The young lord guessed that the fire was from the dragon. He could not imagine what would cause the beast to react with its infernal breath. There was a small spot of hope that it was Lord Penwarden attacking the monster again, but he doubted that the ruler of the lesser landholdings would have the resources to re-equip his remaining men. Jaeme reminded himself that according to Counselor Sejanus, not a single man had been lost in Penwarden's attempt at the serpent. He also recalled that his own forces had not lost a man.

Jaeme counted his brave knights fortunate. Rumor had it that peasants were disappearing daily, wandering into the wood, only to return like men possessed. Or something like that; the stories were always inconsistent and wholly fantastic.

The thought of returning made the young lord wonder about Laela, where his thoughts always returned. He hoped that she would have no trouble finding her way back to Castle Elfwood. He berated himself for allowing her to leave. At the time, the idea that the Druidic Council might be able to help in the battle against the dragon shone with an unarguable light. Now that the druidess was gone, he wished that he had never agreed.

"What help could she bring?" he whispered to himself as he rose from the throne and leaned against the sill of the vaulted window. The light from the dragon's flame left a bright streak of purple across his vision and he blinked so hard his eyes ran with tears. He peered outside the window again, expecting to see another plume of fire. Nothing made itself apparent.

The safety of the Elfwood had always been a major concern of his father's, but other than the obvious reasons of beauty, occasional timber, and the protection it lent against attacks from the west and south, Jaeme could find no reason for the fervent measures taken by his sire to protect the wood.

Jaeme had always thought the druids to be the ultimate guardians of the forest. He shrugged to himself and questioned the danger a dragon might pose to a whole community of druids. Of course, he knew nothing about dragons and assumed them to be invincible. By the same token, he knew little more about druids and assumed them invincible as well.

Through his blurred eyes, Jaeme saw that the fog continued to billow and roil outside the confines of the castle, as if patiently waiting to be invited inside. The black caravan remained immersed in the ocean of mists, and still none of the guards was willing to investigate the train. Occasionally, only the stablehands went near the horses, and it was whispered among their number that the gaunt animals would not eat what was offered. The steeds were malevolent enough to frighten away any subsequent attempts.

The young lord drew back from the window, his imagination creating faceless horrors staring out at him from between the cracks in the iron plating of the lead wagon. Forcing himself to breathe more easily, Jaeme laughed at himself.

''How silly can I be?'' he asked the air, peering down at the stones beneath his feet in shame.

''Your shirt is proof. never make a challenge you cannot finish,'' a familiar, lost voice said from behind. A fold of the bright shirt of punishment was lifted.

Jaeme spun around and tried to fumble the silver sword from its sheath, but it would not come. His head jerked up from where he had stared at the floor, and he saw the eyes of his father upon him.

* * *

Jaeme awoke with a start, still sitting on the throne with the magicked blade lying across his knees. He tried to stand, but found that he was too weak to move. His heart beat so loudly he could hear it in his ears. Breath refused to enter his body.

The young lord closed his eyes, struggling to bring himself up out of the depths of his fear and surprise. The dream had been incredibly real, almost too real to believe it had been anything other than the genuine touch of his father. Now easily pulling the blade from its smooth sheath, Jaeme held the sword up to his face. His eyes gazed back at him darkly, and for a moment he thought his dead sire stared back at him.

"Are you better, my son?"

In his rich burial finery, Richard Mortimer stood before Jaeme, seeming as solid to the new Lord of Elfwood as the sword he held in his hands and as real as the purple flash that continued to streak across his vision. Once again he tried to rise, but his legs still refused to move. He was held fast in his chair by an unseen force that manifested itself in his body as unbearable fatigue.

"I—"

Tears of pain filled Jaeme's eyes, rolling down his face in warm cascades. Every grief that he had ever felt at the death of his father filled his heart and drained his soul. He knew of a thousand words to say to his sire had he the chance again. Now the man stood before him and not a word came to his lips. He did not utter a cry, but his body shook and he clutched the silvered blade to himself as if it would save his life.

"My son, please. Again my time is short, and there is much to tell you."

Jaeme allowed his pain to remain as rivulets on his flesh, making no attempt to wipe them away. He wanted his father to know the full extent of his sorrow, not because the man had died and left the new lord alone and inexperienced, but for respect, and honor, and love. The sword grew hot in his grip.

"What do you mean 'again'?" Jaeme asked. His voice was soft but steady.

Richard Mortimer turned and peered behind him, and the young lord saw nothing more than the doorway. However, the portal was filled with a blackness darker and deeper than any he had seen on even the blackest night. When Mortimer turned back, his face was filled with a mixture of distress and apprehension, something Jaeme found profoundly disturbing. He had never witnessed fear in his father.

"What it is, Father? Let me—"

"There is naught you can do for me, Jaeme," Mortimer interjected, holding up his hand for silence, "for I am truly dead, and only able to speak with you through the magic of the sword."

Jaeme almost threw the weapon down, but found that he could not release his hand from its searing metal. The heat did not damage his flesh; it was, he discovered, an intense sensation of burning rather than the actual thing. The effect was strangely repulsive and comforting at the same time.

"The blade's glamour drew me from my servitude in the Wycham to speak with you when you next slept with it in your hands. There, I met a friend of yours, a Decutonius Consulus," the dead Lord of Elfwood intoned.

"Dec! He's alive! Where is he now? I need him—"

"Jaeme, please!" Richard Mortimer said, peering behind him into the void of the doorway a second time. "I can allow no more interruptions!"

"Yes, Father," Jaeme muttered in respect, as he knew he had done when his sire had been among the living.

"As I said to the mage, there is an evil upon the land that you must destroy. It threatens the whole of the Elfwood and thereby the world."

Jaeme looked up, his eyes filled with confusion at his father's words. "I don't understand."

"Be still and listen. The magic of the blade will not last much longer," Richard Mortimer cautioned. "This evil will devour the life of all things and dance on the bones of the dead. It is uncountably old, and takes no stock in the family or hearth."

Clutching the sword tighter, the young Lord of Elfwood was actually shocked to hear his father speak of the hearth. The man believed the sanctity of the home to be ultimately sacred. Something that threatened it must be truly malevolent.

"Where is this evil, Father?" Jaeme asked, tasting some of the anger he knew his father must feel. "And how may I destroy it?"

The old Lord of Elfwood glanced behind him again, and did not turn back for quite some time. Jaeme was afraid that his father would bolt for the void before there was a chance to say the precious things that still refused to come to his tongue. After a few more unbearable moments, Richard Mortimer finally faced his son.

"The evil is everywhere Jaeme. It is everywhere, and you must enter it to conquer."

The man who spoke to his son from the shadow of the dead turned on his heel and slowly made for the portal of infinite darkness. From the assured stride of his father's steps, Jaeme was sure that he was not going to stop.

"Father. Father! Will the sword allow us to speak again?" he cried, sounding as desperate as a child lost in the night.

"Find the name, my son," Richard Mortimer said, vanishing with haste into the doorway that led to strange lands. "Find the name of the sword."

"Father!"

Jaeme stood up so suddenly that he was forced to brace himself against the sill or fall out the window. His heart continued its racing beat, and he turned and propped himself up against the wall for support, breath ragged.

The sword was still clutched in his right hand. Its metal was hot, but growing cooler in the mundane night air. The sheath was on the stones before the throne.

Tears continued to stain Jaeme's face but he did not utter a sound. By whatever magic the weapon possessed, he had spoken with his dead sire, and the man had told him of an evil so great that the world was in danger. Jaeme was determined to discover the source of this danger.

Straightening himself out, the young lord looked out the window at the black caravan, suppressing a shudder. He wished the train would leave his castle and take the choking fog with it.

"Wishing will not make it happen," he whispered to himself, pushing the matter to the back of his mind. He had a dragon to face, and he was going to muster the force necessary to vanquish the monster.

Jaeme retrieved the scabbard and started to resheathe the sword. He hesitated a moment, tarrying on his own reflection, the reflection that had shown him the eyes of his father. He would never forget the blessed time he had spent alone with his sire.

The young lord left the Great Hall, leaving the throne near the window. The doorway was not filled with stygian darkness, and, like his father, Jaeme did not hesitate as he stepped through to accept his charge.

The dragon must be destroyed.

Chapter 12

DESPITE THE AFFINITY WITH NATURE THAT THE DRUIDS POSSESSED, Laela found herself unable to navigate well through the Elfwood. The fog seemed to have something to do with this, as every time she peered down into it from her place in the skies she would feel the most overpowering vertigo take hold of her. The falling night made the journey even more difficult.

By her guess, the spell of transformation she had cast upon herself was not going to wear off very soon, but Laela felt it prudent to come to ground and change back into her natural form. She was surprised to discover that a moment before she landed, her body shifted and flowed from hawk to human. The ground was hard and cold, bruising her shoulders and back. The wind left her lungs and she gasped for air as the fog continued to roll and curl over her.

Noticing a large rock only a few inches from her head, she sat up abruptly, shocked that she had almost lost her life to an accident. The world swam before her eyes and she blinked to clear the shimmering stars summoned from her laboring breath.

After waiting a few moments, the druidess stood and peered around the area in which she had landed. To her dismay, she found that she was still a good fly from the border of the forest.

"How could I have gotten so lost?" she asked the wind. Her words were swallowed by the sea of mists.

"The fog is said to work evil tricks," a voice answered from behind.

Laela turned and prepared to run, her heart beating fast and her breath shallow again. She saw a strange apparition coalesce out of the fog, someone wearing a heavy cloak with a deep hood.

The druidess reached for a pouch of herbs that she might use for a defensive cantrip, but suddenly realized that she was completely naked; as a bird she could wear no clothing. She had not thought of this before, as she had spent most of her life unclothed, running naked through the unpopulated forests. Now, with this person standing before her, she became very self-conscious.

"I have an extra cloak for you," the apparition said as Laela started to back away into the forest like a frightened woodland spirit. It was a woman who spoke, but her voice was so deep and commanding, it might have passed for a man's.

"Please, take this cloak. I was about to start a fire," the woman uttered, holding a dark bundle out in her hands.

Against her better judgment, Laela stepped forward. A surprisingly dry twig snapped under her right foot. Nudging it with her toe, she discovered a small pile of wood, perfect for a fire, which she'd failed to see because of the fog. She decided that the rock on which she'd nearly brained herself must be this woman's seat.

Taking the preferred garment, Laela said, "Thank you . . ."

"Katherine."

"Thank you, Katherine."

The fabric was coarse and woven from heavy fibres. Although Laela had never donned a suit of armor—no druid ever would—she was sure it couldn't be more restricting than this garment. However, the fog continued its ceaseless vigil over the land, bringing more cold than she wanted to struggle against. At least the cloak was warm.

Flames crackled in the kindling and Katherine soon had a sizable fire going. Sitting on the ground nearby, Laela was forced to pull the hood away from her face because of the waves of heat. Her host did not seem bothered.

"You don't seem alarmed by my—sudden appearance," Laela said.

"I have seen many things in my time. More than most," Katherine replied. The woman sat as still as a statue, and it seemed to Laela that her voice emanated not from the cloak but from all around, from the fog. It made the druidess uneasy in a way she hadn't experienced since a pack of dogs had chased her as a child, tracking her by scent. "Druids are not unknown to me," the woman went on. "And I might add that you do not seem especially surprised by *my* appearance."

Laela felt as though she were being probed for something she could not quite grasp. She decided to be cagey, and replied, "Should I be?"

"Fallen to ground you come across a stranger in the middle of a forest, a forest that you should be able to leave at any time," Katherine stated in a rhetorical tone. "That would seem reason enough to feel a little—trepidation, shall we say?"

The fact that the stranger was correct in everything she said made Laela feel even stronger about simply leaving, running as fast as her legs would carry her through the ramparts of mist. If she could get her bearings, she should be able to leave Elfwood within . . . actually, she was not sure how long it would take her on foot. The fall seemed to have had some adverse effect on her sense of distance.

"As a druid," she began, hoping her voice sounded confident, "I have also seen many things." After a moment's hesitation, she added, "No, I am not *surprised*. Perhaps *wondering* is a better word."

Laela thought the woman shrugged, but there was no way

to tell for sure through the flickering bonfire. "As you will. I am sorry I have nothing to offer in the way of drink."

"That's all right. I am fine."

There was time of silence between the two. Laela was beginning to feel strangely comfortable in the presence of this woman, and she did not understand why. As Katherine herself had pointed out, the druidess should have been at least skeptical about this "chance" encounter. But she wanted to find out why this woman was apparently alone in the forest and willing to bring up the matter of her own trustworthiness.

"Besides, what effect could she have had on me?" Laela muttered to herself.

"I'm sorry?" Katherine said. For the first time, the druidess saw the cloaked figure move, turning.

Laela shook her head. "Nothing. I was just wondering whence you come."

"Ah." The cloak nodded. "As to that, not even I can remember."

"Why is that?" Laela inquired, hoping her voice did not carry the subtle suspicion she felt. She tried to get a closer look at the person inside the cloak, but the fire dazzled her sight and the fog kept her eyes from seeing.

" 'The road makes infants of us all,' " Katherine said, a statement that sounded to the druidess like a quote. " 'We remember nothing of where we have been, only where we desire to go.' A favorite quote of mine, from the Bard."

"I'm afraid I'm not familiar with that one," Laela said, moving to the right of the fire to get a better perspective.

"Nor should you be. But tell me, where were you off to in the form of a hawk?"

"To—to see some friends," Laela returned, changing her statement at the last moment. She doubted that Katherine would let the slip go unnoticed.

"I see," the woman replied, keeping her back straight and her head up like a statue enveloped in grey mist and sackcloth. "You are the druidess Laela of the court of Castle Elfwood, obviously on your way back."

Laela was instantly alarmed. "How do you know—"

Katherine raised her right hand in a gesture of peace. The druidess saw that the fingers were perfectly tapered and the skin whiter than the palest dove. It was the most beautiful hand she had ever seen, and for some reason she felt the virtue of the woman beneath the cloak must exceed even the hand.

"Is it not obvious? Your name is known throughout this land as Lord Jaeme Mortimer's counselor. You were heading in that direction." The woman shrugged again. "A simple conclusion."

Laela saw no reason to confirm the facts that were already apparent. However, she decided not to deny them, either.

"What is Lord Jaeme's demeanor?" Katherine inquired without waiting for the druidess to speak. "Does he take pleasure in his reign?"

The druidess's reply was distant and objective. "I hear that all he takes is the pleasure of ensuring his people's safety."

Katherine turned away from Laela as the young woman finally inched her way around the edge of the fire, frustrating the druidess further. It seemed to her now that this mysterious stranger had some hidden agenda and was trying to gain some information about Jaeme. That meant possible harm to the new lord and potential danger for the Elfwood. Laela felt it was her duty to discover more.

"Are you heading to the castle?" she inquired, hoping her question shrewd.

The woman in sackcloth shrugged again. "Perhaps. I have not yet decided. But as for you, young druidess," Katherine said, suddenly turning and pointing a perfect, commanding finger at Laela, "I suggest you flee these night airs quickly. There is great evil here. Beyond lies a small village where you might find shelter for the night, but even the days are to be avoided!"

Laela was stunned by the statement, unsure of the final meaning of the words. At first, Katherine had been neutral, then sinister, and now she was counsel. The druidess was about to come to a decision, when she heard a yell from behind and the proud cry of a noble horse. Turning, she saw the light of numerous torches closing in like a strangler's hands onto a little patch of darkness.

"Cedric!" she exclaimed, jumping to her feet. Laela spun to face Katherine to ask for assistance in aiding the knight, but the woman was gone, leaving only the dance of the flames behind.

"I cannot kill these louts!" Cedric bellowed to Dec, who fumbled madly through his pouches while trying to maintain his place on his horse. His legs were becoming so tired, he was not sure he could stay on much longer.

"Why not?" the magician shot back, though he agreed with the knight. He finally removed a brittle piece of moss and a pinch of sawdust, almost dropping them both when the horse bucked in response to the shouts of the approaching mob.

Cedric attempted to find a way through the throng, but saw no hope. "They do not know what they do. They don't deserve death!"

The peasants closed their circle and were now only a few paces away. The old knight and the mage saw angry faces in the crowd, eerily illumed by flickering torches. The scene seemed to have been taken from a tome describing the Abyss, one of the most frightening books Dec had ever read.

Cedric shifted the broadsword so the flat of the blade was now the prominent side. He held onto the still-sleeping girl with his other hand. Pele pawed madly at the ground, a trick the knight had taught the horse to frighten bandits and other cowards.

The effect of the huge black horse seemed to work for a moment and the farmers looked to each other for support. Dec could tell by the look in their eyes that they weren't going to stay scared for too long. He closed his eyes to concentrate on his cantrip, though the thought of not seeing the pitchfork or shovel that was going to kill him made him strangely uncomfortable.

The spell he wanted to perform was little more than a prank used by the apprentice magicians at the Magisterium

Lundinium, but he wanted to do it on a much larger scale. He wasn't sure if he would be able to get it to work.

"Dec! What are you doing?" Cedric yelled, his voice hot with anger. Turning to see the odds from behind, he noticed that the mage had his eyes closed and his hands curled in strange positions. "I order you to—!"

"*Cesius lanstrutum*," Dec muttered, clapping his hands together and blowing on the sudden mixture of moss and shavings.

The peasants facing the mage fell to the ground, yelling and grabbing at their bodies. They scratched madly, writhing about with such fervor that Dec was sure they were going to hit their heads on tree stumps or rocks.

"Let's go!" Dec shouted in joy, sure that they were going to live. He was extremely pleased with himself for the quick modification to the itching spell. The words of the high druid had been more than helpful.

Cedric glared from atop his horse like a terrifying vision. Dec shrank back on his horse, realizing that he had alienated himself even further from the old knight's sympathies.

"What was I to do?" he begged. "I'm a magician!"

The peasants watched as their friends tore at their clothes in an attempt to get at whatever irritated their skin. At first, they were frightened, then confused. After a few moments, they were more furious than before.

"Kill the sorcerer!"

The mob pressed forward like a crushing wave from the ocean. Before berating the young man, Cedric forced Pele into a tight turn, making the horse's legs kick outward. A wall of people fell upon themselves to get out of the way of the flashing hooves, while others stumbled as the huge chest of the mount threatened to knock them senseless. In a single motion, Cedric grabbed onto the reins of Dec's horse again and charged through the circle of peasants. Three pitchforks clattered off his armor and a shovel scored a gash in his vambrace, drawing blood across his forearm. He knocked the man with the shovel unconscious with the flat of his sword and kept the rest at bay with a shining sweep of the blade.

Cedric forced Pele into a quick run, nearly jerking the magician from his saddle. Dec hung on for his life, reeling more from the effect of the knight's glare than from fear of the mob.

The peasants were quick to take up the chase. To Dec, their numbers seemed inexhaustible as they kept coming out of the fog, torches burning with only slightly less fire than their gazes. As the two horses came upon a huge tree stump in the middle of the road, Dec turned in time to feel the prong of a pitchfork bite into his thigh. He screamed and kicked out at the man, whose face was invisible in the curling mists. The fork fell away, leaving a bloody trail and white pain.

Cedric forced the horses up and over the obstacle, keeping a firm grip on Rowene. His plan was to keep moving as fast as possible to outdistance the peasants. No matter where he and the mage ended up, it needed to be far enough away from the mob that they would never be able to catch up. He hoped that there were no pit-traps as there had been during his campaign in the Pictish Wastes.

The collective flare of several dozen torches appeared out of the fog too quickly for Cedric to make a proper retreat. He skirted the horses around the arc, swinging the heavy broadsword like a club to strike blows or merely keep the peasants at bay. They yelled in surprise, pain, and anger, but Dec did not hear fear in a single voice. It made him very afraid.

The horses did their best to navigate the rough terrain off the road, but the old knight realized that he would barely be able to walk in this area, let alone lead horses through these trees. Peering behind him, he hoped there might be a way back to the main road. Torches and shouts that became heated whispers in the choking mists returned to crush his hope.

"Why didn't you ride through the hole I made?" Dec implored. The blood ran through his fingers, but he did not complain. If he couldn't have respect in Cedric's eyes for his abilities, he was not going to show any pain and whimper like a child.

The knight stopped scanning the shifting horizon of his vision. "I will not rely on magic for aid," he replied darkly. He felt dishonorable enough the first time that Dec had used his unnatural power to escape the peasants.

"But it *worked*! We were safe!"

"I will not rely on magic for aid," the knight replied again. Dec heard a distinct taint of old prejudice in the man's voice; he hoped one day to melt that barrier.

"All right," Dec said, tearing away a strip of his robe. "What do we do now?" He tied the cloth around his thigh as a temporary bandage, knowing he would have to be looked after by a chirurgeon soon.

"We must continue to move through the forest. Perhaps we can find a stream or another path—"

Cedric was knocked off his horse as a sledgehammer slammed into his back so hard that another dent appeared in the thick plate of his armor. He had not let go of the sleeping child and had the foresight to shield the girl's body with his own as he rolled. Though he was loath to admit it to himself, this was not the first time he had been unhorsed.

Dec attempted to jump off his mount to help his friend, but a thousand hands suddenly grabbed him and pinned him to the ground. There were no torches this time and he was strangely relieved to discover that he would not be burned at the stake. Then he was slugged in the face by a heavy fist, and light finally appeared in the fog. . . .

The old knight released the child just in time to shield her from the next attack. He was forced to his face again and guessed that the man with the hammer was somewhere behind and to the left. Cedric swung the broadsword in a wild arc, catching something soft on the tip of the blade. To his satisfaction, there was a loud scream.

"Die, wizard!" somebody hissed angrily.

Cedric rose from his place on the ground and charged toward the voice and the sound of flesh beating flesh. No sooner had he got to his feet than he was knocked backward, the hammer striking him just below the collar line. The armor shattered and sent splinters of hot metal through his flesh. He lashed out again with his sword as the world swam in darkness, but found no mark.

The hammer crashed down again, on his right shoulder. The blow sent the sword spinning off to be swallowed by the hungry mists. Cedric could no longer feel the right side of his body.

The man with the sledge yelled in sudden fear, dropping his makeshift weapon and running. The men holding Dec were still enjoying their game when the first of their number was thrown twenty feet to disappear into the fog. The man raining blows on the senseless magician lost most of the skin on his back, then fell unconscious from the pain.

Roaring, the bear lumbered toward the peasants who were the last to leave the mage's battered body. The mob quickly lost its appetite for murder. Their numbers dwindled quickly, the torches receding at the speed of a good run.

Laela bent down near Dec, peering through the curling mists to inspect his wounds. Seeing that he was unconscious but not near death, she raced to Cedric's side.

She helped the old knight lie down on the ground and tried to strip him of his armor, but the clasps could not be reached through the battered mail. The druidess waved her hand in front of the man's face, muttering a few words of a simple healing spell she had learned from Myrna.

Cedric's eyes fluttered open, fixing Laela with a gaze that made her shrink back in surprise. ''Where is Rowene?'' he asked. His voice was still strong, though his body had been shattered.

Confused for a moment, Laela searched around in the area. The girl she found was still asleep, though in such a way as to make her guess the sleep was not natural. The druidess held the girl up for Cedric to see.

''Good,'' he muttered, closing his eyes. After a deep breath, he said, ''We must get her to Castle Elfwood.''

Chapter 13

JAEME KNEW THAT ANY ONE OF HIS COUNSELORS WOULD HAVE TOLD him that to leave the castle completely undefended was foolish. At the moment, he doubted that anything less than his entire muster, including the soldiers from *all* the surrounding territories, would have any chance against the dragon.

After he had left the Great Hall and the living memory of his father, the young Lord of Elfwood had ordered each of his heralds to demand the return of all men to arms. In fact, the majority of the nobles and their soldiers had been prepared and ready to engage the legendary serpent a second time. After seeing the huge gout of flame in the night, from a distance that would have taken a fast horse more than a day to cover, Jaeme was not so sure the men should be so eager.

The newly re-formed and re-equipped company met outside the castle walls, well away from the pool of darkness created by the black-iron wagon train. Counselor Teves had been nervous about the mysterious caravan and did not want to be left alone with it. Jaeme knew that he, like many others in the castle, had refused to leave because they did not want to step anywhere near the wagons or the malevolent black horses. The new lord had figured that if the travellers in the caravan had been waiting for something, they would have appeared by now. After all, this was not the first time that the castle had been left defenseless.

Sir Kipp arrived before most of the other nobles. "I had a feeling that today you would want our help again," he said with a dashing smile. He carried his helmet in his hand, and Jaeme saw with concern that it had a huge dent in it.

The knight followed the young lord's gaze and laughed. "'Tis true. I fell from my horse," he said loudly and good-naturedly. "We'll see who falls this time, eh, Jaeme?"

Before Jaeme could comment, Sir Kipp rode off to confer with Desmond, who had recently arrived with a wagonload of supplies and weapons.

The new day was even greyer than usual, as if the fog were making a concerted effort to confound the gathering force. The new Lord of Elfwood peered back through the mists at the serpentine line of the black caravan and wondered if the people inside cared about the fog, or anything at all. For a moment, he again considered approaching the train. The idea made him shrink back into his saddle, and not even the silvered blade could bring him solace.

Soldiers slowly gathered in the main road leading back to the castle. Their sergeants and captains barked out quick orders that were easily lost in the fog and the clatter of spears and swords. Jaeme turned back to face the approach of his men-at-arms and discovered that he did not feel the same fear for their lives as he had before. Now there was no *fear*, though concern remained in his heart. Since speaking with his dead sire, Jaeme knew that the survival of the world depended on the destruction of the evil in the land. For that, it seemed acceptable to lead his men into battle.

"What thoughts, my lord?" Desmond said at his side.

"Tell me," Jaeme replied, continuing to stare out at the

growing mass of soldiers. "When does a man know he has a cause worthy of other men's lives."

The young lord waited for an answer for some time. In the interim, the sound of weapons checked and resheathed, the calls of captains, colored the question with a palette of war.

"I think he may know it when the other men are willing to follow," his mentor finally answered. "These men may be soldiers, but they are still men. They make their own choices."

"By that token," Jaeme began, his voice sounding skeptical in his ears, "this cause must be doubly worthy."

Desmond shifted in his saddle and shrugged. "Nobody said it wasn't, my lord."

Jaeme turned and stared sharply at the man next to him, but Desmond's face held no hint of sarcasm. In a way, the young lord had hoped his trainer had been teasing him, as that would have confirmed his own suspicions about himself and his inability to lead. Now that the man had said the cause was just, Jaeme would have to accept the responsibility without the armor of self-deprecation to shield him and give him an excuse in case something went amiss.

"When shall we leave?" the young lord asked.

"Whenever you give the word, my lord."

"Very well," Jaeme said, turning one last time toward Castle Elfwood and the black caravan. "Let us ride!"

The assembly of infantry and cavalry moved more slowly than Jaeme would have liked, but the fog was treacherous, filling the deepest gullies so that they appeared no deeper than a footprint. A few men along the way stumbled so badly they had to return home with twisted ankles and bruised heads.

Along the way, scouts and messengers were sent to the lords that had not been contacted in the morning. There were many nobles who did not add their available forces to the Elfwood contingent, and Jaeme ordered Desmond to make a note about them. The trainer also made favorable note of those landholders who did willingly lend their support.

"Do you think this sortie wise, my lord?" Sir Kipp inquired respectfully, still holding his battered helmet.

"Why do you ask, Sir Kipp?"

The knight paused before replying. "Well, my lord," he began haltingly, "you leave your home defenseless. What of the scoundrels waiting for a chance like this to—"

"I do not think I have aught to fear, Sir Kipp. As before, if the other nobles desired to take Elfwood whilst I am gone, they would have done it the first time," Jaeme replied.

"Very wise, my lord," the knight said. He bowed his head once and rode on to confer with the other nobles. Jaeme guessed that they had all had the same question in their minds.

It seemed to Jaeme that the column was making much worse time than should be expected, even for a mass troop movement travelling in fog. He found that if he stared back hard enough through the heavy mist, he could still see his home and castle. He was about to discuss this matter with Desmond, but decided that seeing Elfwood could be little more than a wishful thought affecting the sight.

Of wishful thoughts, he hoped that Laela had not run into any mishaps. He was worried that she had not returned before the small army left to fight the dragon. In case she did arrive after he was gone, he ordered counselor Leker, the most trusted of the three advisors, to give her the exact direction and ultimate destination of the soldiers. He told himself that if she were still travelling in the form of a hawk or some other bird she might fly over the formation and land; that would make everything so much easier. Of course, he knew that because of the ocean of mist, she might fly over them all and not notice a thing. His body tensed at that idea.

The day wore on, and finally the wash of the sun set below the line of the cliffs at the sea's edge. The land was bathed in darkness and cold, forcing the column to halt its march at the edge of the Elfwood, still more than a day's journey to Wycham Wood, where Jaeme knew the dragon must be waiting. He ordered Sir Kipp to have the men make camp.

"Should we not press on through the night?" Sir Kipp asked, squinting into the gathering dusk to determine the distance to their ultimate destination.

"I think not," Jaeme replied, reining Firebrand to a halt. "The men must be in the best possible condition when we engage the dragon again."

Sir Kipp reined his own mount to a stop near Jaeme and pulled out a piece of parchment so old that the corners flaked away as it was unrolled.

"What is that?" the young lord inquired curiously.

"A treatise, my lord. About dragons."

Jaeme was surprised and impressed. None of his advisors had discovered anything of the sort in Elfwood's archives. "What does it say?"

Clearing his throat, Sir Kipp brought the scroll up closer to his eyes so he might read it in the failing light. "'Written by Sir Walter Everett Kipp upon the arrival of his family to this land in the year of our Lord'—I'm sorry, the parchment fades here."

"That's all right," Jaeme said, genuinely interested both in what Sir Walter Everett Kipp had to say and in the contemporary Sir Kipp's lineage. "Please continue."

"'An accounting of dragons and their kind as witnessed therein by this scribe. . . . And having seen the great monster lay waste to the crops and animals of the farm, did I send my noblest knights to do battle with the vile serpent, only to have them return much injured. Therein did I set upon a plan to flush the fell beast from the wood where it hid and take it unawares in the open.'"

"And?" Jaeme probed, anxiously waiting for more.

"That is basically all, my lord," Sir Kipp answered, rerolling the scroll and returning it to a heavy iron case.

"But the idea of flushing the dragon ocurred to you to be a good idea."

The noble nodded his agreement. "We have no impetus when our lines are scattered through the wood."

"I see your excellent point, Sir Kipp. Very commendable,'' Jaeme added, something he guessed his father would have said. ''Please take as many men as you deem necessary to implement this plan.''

''Thank you, my lord,'' the knight replied. Rotating his horse expertly in a tight circle, Sir Kipp rode off to make his plans.

Jaeme sighed out loud, thankful that nobody was near to ask him what was wrong. He did not doubt that the noble's plan would succeed; he just hoped it would be enough.

''Heard there was a place down south that wasn't covered in this cursed fog,'' the merchant said to Jaeme as he and another man labored to push a small wagonload of goods along the road.

''And the others behind you?'' the young lord inquired, indicating the line of people who followed.

''They're from my village, too,'' the man replied. ''We're the only brave ones. Bad crops, strange voices, the cold. And the dragon! The rest prefer to cower in their homes and wait for the darkness to get them.''

Jaeme nodded sagely. He had removed his armor and other accouterments that would identify him as the new Lord of Elfwood. When the scouts had told him of a small column of peasants, farmers, and merchants plodding along the main road, he took the opportunity to turn his inexperience as lord into an asset for once.

''Would you like to sell that shirt?'' the merchant asked.

Jaeme glanced down at himself for a moment and remembered that he still wore the shirt of punishment. He would have liked to rid himself of it, but doubted that this was an acceptable way of doing so.

''No, thank you anyway,'' he said, turning Firebrand, who had also been stripped, back toward his army.

''One last thing,'' the man said with a sage nod of his own. ''Don't go near Penwarden. I hear there's trouble.''

The merchant winked and Jaeme winked back, though he hadn't a clue as to what the man was getting at. Putting it to the back of his mind for the moment, he rode back to the nobles and men-at-arms, who were resting only a few hundred paces away. The fog was so heavy and stultifying that the army could not be seen from just off the main road.

Night was fast approaching, and Jaeme's contingent of men was still nowhere near Castle Penwarden. It seemed that nobody had any sense of direction, the rampart of mists making map travel difficult at best and the actual travelling nearly impossible. There were many times when the formations broke up within feet of each other because the men could not keep track of where their leaders were placed.

"What did you discover, my lord?" Desmond asked, holding Jaeme's mail up like a nightshirt.

The young lord slowed his horse and jumped off before the steed had come to a halt. He was feeling very frustrated. After preparing himself to engage the dragon a second time, hopefully aided by Penwarden's troops, being stalled by nothing more than bad weather was grating.

Jaeme slipped his arms into his armor and allowed the trainer to buckle him back up. "The citizens of this realm fear the fog, the dark, and the dragon. They think heading south with save them."

"Perhaps they are right," Desmond offered.

"What do you suggest we do, Desmond? Move everyone?" the young lord snapped.

"Please excuse me, my lord," the trainer muttered. "I meant no offense."

Jaeme took several deep breaths and allowed the man who had taught him the meaning of honor and discipline to finish dressing him. "Desmond—" he began plaintively.

The trainer snapped the last buckle loudly shut. "No need to apologize, Jaeme. You are the lord."

"And you are my friend, and my father's friend," Jaeme answered, relieved that he would not have to spend the rest of his life restoring his relationship with the man. "I believe he once said that if one man in all the land possessed tolerance, it was you."

Jaeme's mentor gave a short laugh and made sure the armor was in place. "He was speaking of my ability to drink."

Both men laughed, which the young lord thought was a

strange sound in the gathering darkness. For a moment, he hoped that the mirth would cause the mists to lift, but he was disappointed.

It was not much longer until the dull orb that was the sun sank below the horizon, leaving the land in gloom and poor humor. The campfires of the soldiers were quiet, the men eating listlessly. Jaeme saw that much of their time was spent staring out into the shifting mists; from his own experience, he did not envy whatever sorrow-filled portion of their lives they were reliving. Even the tents of the nobles were somber.

Jaeme wished that his friends were near him, and wondered if Laela had received the message he left. The young lord fought another bout with regret and doubt. After all, if the army with all its maps was unable to find the way to Penwarden, something relatively simple, what reason was there to assume that a woman in the form of a bird could find the army?

Jaeme re-examined his thoughts and realized how unlikely it was for a woman to be in the form of a bird in the first place. The thought heartened him strangely.

The new Lord of Elfwood went back near his tent, where his squire was busily polishing armor. Jaeme saw that Skyler was shivering in the unnaturally cold night air.

"Skyler! Go back inside before you catch your death," he commanded, knowing that the boy would immediately argue.

"All right," Skyler mumbled. To Jaeme's surprise, the squire dropped everything and stumbled back into the relative warmth of the tent. Jaeme stared after him in concern, picking up his equipment and setting the pieces on their holding stakes. He figured that the cold must be affecting the boy more than the men.

He was about to go inside and ask what the trouble was, when he heard a distinctive sound, of carts and wheels rolling across soft terrain. The sound was strangely familiar. When the great shape melted out of the fog, its stretched and weathered tarp captured by the wan firelight of the soldiers, Jaeme remembered: it was the sound of the black wagons.

However, what approached was only a single wagon made of mundane wood and cloth. Jaeme found that his hand had instinctively gone to the silver sword at his side. He swallowed hard on fear-tainted bile and felt his heart pound hard in his chest. A few of the heralds still awake approached the wagon and waited for it to stop. After a moment, a cloaked figure stepped down off the buckboard, lashing the reins to a hand brake.

Jaeme watched the figure leave the wagon and at first thought it might be a monk on some religious errand. He had also heard of some traders wearing similar robes to protect them from inclement weather, some kind of guild-approved regulation outfit. This traveller, though, was neither monk nor trader. When she pulled her hood back, Jaeme beheld a face so beautiful, with skin so pale, he wanted to have it engraved in stone forever.

''Good eve, to you, sir,'' the woman said, her voice dark and rich. ''My name is Katherine.''

''You say you are travelling toward the coast?'' Jaeme inquired over a mug of hot mead. Katherine sat near to him on a log by the bonfire. The woman's alabaster face seemed to catch every flash of fire and steal its warmth.

''Yes, then south.''

''What will you find?'' Sir Kipp inquired openly with a smile, eating a piece of chicken cooked on a nearby spit. Jaeme would have liked to eat as well, but the mysterious woman's quiet nobility made him watch his manners and remain on his best behavior. Eating, under the circumstances, seemed out of the question.

Katherine did not answer at first. She stared into the fire in a way that made the young lord think she was communing with the flame. Presently, she broke the spell and softly replied, ''I have relatives there.''

''In truth?'' the knight said, interested. ''Perhaps I know of them. My family has a long lineage from that land.''

''I do doubt it, my lord. My family lives in the mountains and has no truck with the outside world.''

‘‘Yourself excepted,’’ Jaeme interjected, sitting up straighter.

The woman fixed the young lord with a cool gaze, and nodded in humble confirmation. Jaeme tried to think of something else to say, but nothing came to mind. Fortunately, Katherine went on, ‘‘I have had trouble following any path on my travels, as do the others on the road.’’

‘‘As do we all, my lady,’’ Jaeme quipped. He took a drink of the heavy mead and let the liquor trickle slowly down his throat and warm his chest.

‘‘I have grown afraid to ride through these lands—’’

‘‘Have you no escort?’’ Sir Kipp asked incredulously. He sat up with indignation and added, ‘‘Perhaps you would allow one of my household guards to—’’

‘‘Thank you for your offer, sir, but I have others awaiting me further up the road,’’ Katherine interjected in a manner so final that Sir Kipp was left with nothing else to say, causing Jaeme to smile into his mug. He hoped he would not be noticed.

Desmond took a drink of his mead as well and offered, ‘‘Then you are heading in the direction of Elfwood.’’

Katherine nodded into the fire again and said, ‘‘That would seem to be true.’’

‘‘Then allow me to give you permission to stay at Castle Elfwood for as long as you wish,’’ Jaeme said, putting his mug down on the ground. He was happy to at last be able to do something for this woman other than give his sympathies to her travel woes.

For the first time, Katherine smiled. It was a warm smile, yet at the same time as cold and impenetrable as the fog itself. Her eyes, twin pools of obsidian, were to Jaeme’s thinking, the antithesis of his father’s silver blade.

‘‘Thank you, my lord,’’ the woman said gravely, bowing her head. She rose from her place in the circle and began to gracefully gather her robes about her.

‘‘Before you leave, please let me give you my word in writing—’’

‘‘The hospitality of Elfwood is known even in my land,’’ Katherine interjected.

Jaeme held up an apologetic hand. ''And I hope that I might someday visit your land under less trying circumstances. But these same events force unusual measures, and not everyone is welcome. I am sorry and hope you understand and forgive.''

Katherine bowed her head again, and Jaeme thought she favored him with a slight smile. Her perfect hands lifted the heavy cowl back over her face and she started to walk off toward her wagon.

''One last matter, my lord,'' she said, turning momentarily, her voice made even softer by the cloak. ''I believe I met your friends on the road not a mile from here, to the west.''

Jaeme's eyes went wide with excitement. She could only mean Dec and Sir Cedric. With the knight's help, the young lord was sure that his force would be able to bargain with Penwarden and defeat the dragon. He walked away from the bonfire, heading toward the tent of the scouts, the hope in his heart mingled with the satisfaction that he had met his first real diplomatic challenge and overcome it admirably.

Chapter 14

''JAEME!''

Laela ran into the young lord's arms and hugged him forcefully, wishing only that his armor did not stand in the way of the joy she wished to express at having found him again.

For his part, Jaeme felt much the same way. He was glad both for himself and the safety of his friends.

''We were told that you would be this way,'' he murmured in the druidess's ear. He was careful not to catch her cloak in the angles of his vambraces or mesh of his gauntlets.

''By who?'' Laela asked, holding him out at arm's length. ''We haven't seen anyone for quite some time.''

Jaeme vaguely gestured behind him. ''The diplomat, Katherine.''

Laela's hands dropped to her sides and she took a step back away from Jaeme in fear. The young lord was completely bewildered by his friend's reaction, and wondered what he might have said to upset her so.

''What did she say?'' the druidess asked, feeling again

the chill in her heart that had momentarily been dispelled by Jaeme's fervent embrace.

"Nothing." Jaeme shrugged, still confused and hoping to find a reason for the woman's strange behavior. "She said she had seen you along this way earlier. And that she was heading in the direction of the castle."

"Why does that give me a bad feeling?" Laela asked rhetorically. Staring out into the fog, she imagined she could see the woman's perfect face smiling with both regret and triumph.

Jaeme heard the question and it only added to his confusion. He had found nothing sinister about the woman, and the fact that she was heading toward Elfwood seemed nothing more than a coincidence. "Is there something you know about her that I did not discern?"

Laela shrugged, moving to take the young lord's arm and lead him back to Dec and Cedric. "I don't know, Jaeme. There is more to her than what appears on the surface. Where is the girl Sir Cedric and Dec found?" she added.

Jaeme pointed toward a small band of army surgeons who were examining Rowene for any signs of injury. They were obviously perplexed by her behavior.

"What happened to her?" the young lord whispered.

"I do not know. I have not had the chance to inquire of Cedric."

The mage and the old knight were also being attended to by the chirurgeons who had just pried off Cedric's heavy armor and were treating his wounds. In the dim flicker of lamplight, Jaeme saw that there was a great deal of blood but the wounds themselves were superficial.

"It is remarkable, Sir Cedric, that with the dents in your armor you still live," Jaeme remarked, releasing himself from the druidess's embrace for a moment to bend down and speak to the older man. "Did you encounter the dragon again?"

"Yes, my lord, but these clouts are from the hand of a smith, not the fury of the serpent," Cedric replied. Words like the ones Jaeme had spoken, full of good nature and concern, were something the knight sorely missed from the old days of chivalry. He did not cherish the idea of returning to his place at Penwarden. However, there was something more important on his mind.

"The girl Rowene, my lord. Where is she?"

"Do not fear, Sir Cedric. She will be taken care of and taken back to Elfwood immediately. I'll see to that." Jaeme nudged the old knight's mail and said, "Next time, be sure you have your armor off before the man attempts repairs!"

Jaeme and Cedric laughed at the same time, but the old knight was suddenly racked by fits of coughing that brought blood to his lips. "Forgive me, my lord. I fear the injuries may be deeper than these good men suspect."

"I have performed some minor healings upon him, but I think that he may be right. My magics are not potent enough to cure all his wounds," Laela whispered in Jaeme's ear when he had stood back up and accepted her arm again.

The mention of magic reminded Jaeme of the druidess's urgent errand. "Your mission! What did you find?"

"The Druidic Council gave me a potent weapon against dragons," Laela replied softly, not wishing anyone else to hear and thus be lulled into a false sense of security. "It is a type of charming that you might have heard about in legends and fantasies."

"How is Dec?" Cedric interrupted, wiping away the blood flecking his thick black beard with the back of his hand. "He is brave, but received quite a beating."

"I am fine, Sir Cedric," the young mage replied, appearing out of the fog. "The surgeons helped me with some of the smaller cuts and abrasions, but they fear I may have a permanent scar," he added, tracing a line with his index finger above his right eye all the way to his hairline.

The old knight sat up on his elbow and nodded, brushing away the attempts of the busy chirurgeons to keep him on his back until their work was done. "In this case, Sir Mage, that scar is a mark of honor."

Dec swelled with pride. It seemed to him that the moment stretched on forever, making him uncomfortable under the approving, and apparently amused, stares of Laela and Jaeme. However, it was the first true compliment that the old knight had given Dec, and he was going to savor that moment as long as possible. He was so happy, he no longer felt the throbbing of his forehead.

"Yes, well . . ." he muttered, bowing his head to keep his smile hidden. Jaeme suddenly remembered that the mage had abandoned his post, but the lord decided to let the matter drop. There were obviously too many extenuating circumstances.

"Jaeme! Jaeme!" someone yelled from behind. The young lord turned and saw Desmond running up the slope to where the travellers had been discovered. Jaeme had ordered the trainer and the men-at-arms to keep moving forward, and that meant Desmond must have run nearly the entire distance, a feat Jaeme doubted he himself could perform.

"What is it, Desmond?"

"Castle Penwarden, my lord," the trainer husked, nearly out of breath. "We have found it, and they attack!"

The troops of Castle Elfwood had halted just outside bow range of the castle, maintaining a shield wall and erecting bales of hay taken from the surrounding fields to act as further protection. The men of Penwarden were loosing bolts with wild abandon. Jaeme doubted that one of them had any sanity remaining. For the moment, the fog was not as opaque as it had been on the journey, though the cold remained to haunt the bones of the men.

"Why do they continue to fire at us?" the young lord inquired both of Desmond and Cedric, who had beaten out most of the dents in his armor himself so he might be more comfortable. "We are obviously out of range."

"I do not know," the trainer replied. "They started the moment we arrived, and some of the other men suspect that they had started long before anyone appeared, firing blind. They called us 'devils.'"

"'Tis strange behavior, to be sure," Cedric put in quietly. "They act like men possessed."

"Or men frightened out of their wits," Dec offered. He considered using some kind of spell that would give him the ability to see at a distance through the fog, but did not make the attempt for fear it would offend the old knight and ruin the previous moment's glory. He told himself that there probably wasn't anything to see in any case.

Jaeme turned to Laela, who was preparing a poultice to place on Cedric's and Dec's wounds, a mixture she said would reduce the swelling of their more superficial cuts and contusions. The young lord took a moment to reflect on how beautiful she was, and it pained him to remember that he had let her go off on her own into the treacherous fog. "What do you think, Laela?" he asked.

The druidess looked up from her work with a start, then turned back to finish applying the strong-smelling paste to a strip of cloth. "I think Dec is right. They fear something. I can smell it from here," she answered, hanging the cloth on a nearby branch to let some of the moisture run out. Walking up to join the others, she pointed toward the castle. "See how they huddle in bunches and point in different directions. These are not the actions of rational men."

The men were all amazed at the druidess's abilities to see so clearly across the distance, let alone be actually able to smell the scent of fear in the air from the castle. Jaeme felt a thrill of pride that this woman was both his friend and counsellor, and hopefully more.

"How do you suggest we approach them for parley?" the young lord asked of Laela, though he turned to face everyone and waited for a reply.

There were no immediate answers as each, including Jaeme, came up with solutions that were quickly eliminated. Jaeme thought that a show of the banner of Elfwood might be enough to convince the archers to halt their fire, but if the Lords of Penwarden had any designs at all on Elfwood Castle, it would be the perfect opportunity to ensure its fall. Cedric had a similar idea, but he wanted to storm Penwarden in a show of strength and thereby humble the archers into submission.

Dec continued to think of new spells to cast, perhaps something to put everyone to sleep or to make it rain, or even a fireball to melt the walls and open a breach through which the glorious armies of Castle Elfwood could enter, but none of those options seemed particularly viable. He doubted that any of his spells would have the necessary range; he wished he had paid more attention in class.

After a great deal of consideration, Laela offered a solution. Though she doubted Jaeme would agree to it, there seemed to be little choice.

"I could change myself into a bird, fly inside, and confront Penwarden directly," she blurted out for everyone to hear. Arguments pro and con, broke out.

"No!" the young lord yelled, his voice sounding very final. The look of pain in his dark eyes penetrated deep into Laela's heart.

"Yes!" Dec shouted, snapping his fingers in understanding. He thought the plan brilliant.

"No!" Cedric exclaimed. He was horrified by the idea that this beautiful young woman with whom he felt more than a certain affinity might practice magic to the point where she would desecrate her body.

"Sensible," Desmond murmured. Though his voice was low, Jaeme could still hear it over the din of the others' vociferations. "Makes perfect sense, my lord."

"No!" Jaeme repeated with a chopping motion of his hand. He had gotten Laela back safely from her trip to the Druidic Council and he was not going to lose her again. "Absolutely out of the question."

"But Jaeme, it's brilliant! That way she can get to Penwarden directly and convince him to stop," Dec said, waving his arms in excitement. The mage himself would have given anything to be able to change his form into that of an bird, or better yet, he told himself, a creature like a dragon.

"Coerce is more like it," Desmond added. "I doubt that Penwarden will be willing to talk if he and his men are as frightened as they seem. And you do require the enlistment of his aid to fight the dragon."

The young lord had hoped his trainer would not utter those words, though he knew they were inevitable. The shirt of punishment was cold, and wet from sweat beneath his armor, a reminder of what it meant to be headstrong and foolish. He wondered just how much he needed Penwarden's aid and what would happen if the man could not be convinced. Turning, he stared out over his massed troops, barely visible through the choking mists. They were grand, but against a dragon, would they be enough?

''What of your spell from the Council?'' Jaeme inquired of Laela, hearing his voice lose a measure of its previous heat. ''If you are injured or killed, what good will it do us then?''

Laela folded her arms across her heart, preparing to make her stand. ''There is no guarantee that the Charming will work. There is no guarantee that when approached, Penwarden will be willing to grant us aid. Since we have nothing to operate on except suppositions, I suggest that we attempt to make the best of our men-at-arms and other forces.''

Desmond nodded in satisfaction. ''Ably put.''

Jaeme's shoulders slumped now that he knew he was defeated. Laela's argument made perfect sense and made him feel perfectly horrible. As lord of the land, he knew he could order her to stay, but most likely she would say something like, ''I am a member of the Druidic Council and take no orders from you!'' as she had before. It was one of the many things about her that he found so incredibly lovely.

''You may leave when you have finished tending to Sir Cedric and Dec,'' the young lord murmured, staring out across the field to the castle where the madmen of Penwarden continued to fire their arrows at phantoms in the mists.

The druidess saw that she had hurt Jaeme, and though she wanted to console him and convince him that this plan was the best, she guessed that he needed to be alone and sort things out for himself. Without another word, she went back to her drying poultices.

Cedric ground his teeth in anger, knowing that this was the only emotion left to him when he could not understand the ways of magic. He admired the woman's nobility and spirit, though he could not imagine why she would give herself so fully to sorcery. Laela was saying that she could change into a bird and that was too heinous a sin to imagine; the old knight suddenly realized that he could not recall where the bear had gone after saving him and Dec from the hands of the peasants.

"Don't touch this. It will fall off on its own," the red-haired woman said sternly. Cedric found that the poultice had been applied to his neck, where the rigid collar armor had shattered under the blow of the sledgehammer. He saw that Dec sported a similar piece of cloth on his forehead. The herbs cooled the fire around his throat that threatened infection.

"Thank you, my lady," he grumbled, touching the cloth gingerly.

The druidess put her lips close to the tall knight's ear and whispered, "I know you do not like the ways of magic, Sir Knight. I assure you that there is no evil in my ability."

Laela had felt it necessary to say something to the man or he might continue to grind his teeth until there was nothing left. She was not sure for whose sake she spoke more, his or her own. She merely hoped that Cedric would be able to accept her, and perhaps Dec, more readily.

"Thank you for your candor, my lady," Cedric whispered back. Her fiery mane of hair reminded him of another's from a long time ago, but he ignored that for the moment and added, "There is much history between myself and the way of magic that cannot be ignored."

"I do not ask you to ignore it, only accept *us* for the moment."

Cedric nodded reluctantly. The one thing he had been able to rely on for so many years was his unswerving values. Now, though, he was forced to admit that, for this once, his values did not apply.

"There is one other thing I must ask you, Sir Cedric," Laela continued nervously. She was not sure why she was bringing this matter to light, or what she hoped to gain by its exposure, but she had to know, for the memory of her parents and the sake of herself. "Did you once love a woman like myself, from the Elfwood?"

The question burned into Cedric's soul. The girl was

correct, and looking at her now, he saw that she could be none other than the daughter of the woman he had once loved and left because she lived in the ways of magic. Mixed memories of happiness and sorrow flowed through him, and for the first time, because he beheld the daughter that could have been his own, Sir Cedric cried a single tear.

Entering the castle was not difficult for Laela, though she found that the better marksmen of the keep were more than willing to put aside their fears for a moment's distraction at hunting birds.

When she arrived, she could not decide if she should drop the spell. There were certain advantages to being a person and others to being a hawk. After espying the high towers and windows of the keep, she resolved to maintain her borrowed form.

Having landed in the main courtyard near the inner wall of the castle proper, Laela thought that the best route to go would be from the heights downward. The only castle she had ever visited was Elfwood, and she hoped that the architecture here was similar. She took to wing and flew swiftly to the topmost window.

Peering inside, she found nothing of interest. It appeared to be some kind of chamber, but for whom or for what, she could not decide. The next window over held nothing more of interest.

The next floor down boasted something she had never seen—a beautiful bedroom with a bed that had a silken canopy supported by four posts, one in each corner. There were also two huge mirrors in the room. The only mirrors she had seen before were held in the hand or her simple reflection in ponds.

The druidess wanted to tarry awhile and inspect this bedroom, but knew there was no time to lose. With regret, she soared to the next tower over to the right, wheeling in the air long enough to determine the relative strengths of Penwarden's contingent and the army of Elfwood. The men of this keep were obviously tired, judging by the way they slumped over the ramparts when they weren't firing madly at phantoms. Laela spent a long moment gliding and trying to remember the location of the Great Hall in Castle Elfwood. She came to the conclusion that, like Elfwood, Penwarden's hall would be located where there would probably be no windows to the outside. If there were any at all, they would most likely be decorative and closed.

Her guess was correct. Using her beak and the flexibility of her smaller form, the druidess forced her way between the crack in the main door, which she thought large enough to allow several horses standing abreast to enter. There was very little activity inside, since most of the men were defending the keep. However, all the torches were lit, as if the fortress were owned by a small child who was afraid of the dark.

Senses sharp, Laela heard approaching footsteps from a side corridor and darted on her claws to hide behind a nearby pillar.

"The men grow tired, my lord," an opulently dressed man in purple velvet complained with wide gestures.

"Better than growing dead," the other returned acidly. "Remember what happened when we let up the attack the first time."

"Of course, my lord, but the men—"

"—Are under my command, and I command them to continue! Keep those bastards away from *my* castle!"

Laela had no doubt that the second man was Lord Penwarden. She had heard nothing about the man, but she could tell simply from the way he treated others that he was not going to be easy to convince. The druidess continued to watch the men's movements, waiting for them to enter the door at the end of the hall, which she hoped led to the great hall.

Stepping out into the open, Lord Penwarden took a sudden left turn and his advisor took a right, confounding Laela. She quickly took to the air in a panic before realizing that the sound of her flight would immediately alert anyone nearby. She guessed there was a chance that changing back into human form might aid her at the moment, but if she failed in her mission, she would need a way to escape the keep.

Laela saw no other option as she wheeled back about and shot out through the main door. Staying close to the wall, she peeked into every window as she shot past, her vision greatly improved while a hawk. She saw nothing more than a few servants scurrying back and forth between the rooms.

Returning to the first tower, the druidess rested beside the window of the beautiful bedroom. She looked back out over the open field between the castle and Jaeme's forces and saw, with her heightened vision, that not a single man dared cover the gap. The look on the young lord's face was a mix of concern and anxiousness.

"Got you!" a voice cried from behind. Laela was immediately grappled in such a way that she could neither peck nor claw at her captor.

"This is a good omen!" Lord Penwarden said to his prize. "A hawk so fine could never be bought in the market, and full of spirit as well!"

Laela did not like being referred to as "full of spirit," but at the moment she could find no way out of her dilemma. The lord of the castle was silent as he searched about the room for somewhere to hold the bird captive. He gave up after a moment and shifted Laela under his arm, still in a position where she could not escape. The druidess felt something wrap around her feet, then her wings.

"You'll keep for a while," Penwarden muttered between breaths of careful exertion. He gently laid his new hawk on a nearby table and took one last look out the window.

"Some day I'll use you, if we ever get out of this hell," he added, turning to face Laela again. "We opened our gates and my people died. They came out of the fog to curse our names! Who knows what's real and what's fancy, eh? Eh?"

The man wagged his finger threateningly in front of Laela's beak, giving her the sudden urge to snap at it. She changed her mind and let the lord speak.

"First the dragon, then the devils! What shall be next?" he asked the air, holding his arms out and slowly spinning.

Laela continued silent, torn between sympathy for the man's obvious fear of recent events and revulsion for his sickened state of mind. Penwarden continued to spin until he suddenly dropped to his bed, bringing a hand up to cover his brow.

"Why couldn't I be Lord of Elfwood? I'd be good. I'd be just. I just want to sleep."

With his last word, Lord Penwarden began to snore loudly. The druidess could not imagine how many days the man had been awake from fear of losing his life to "devils," but she guessed from his lack of washing it had been quite some time.

Penwarden awoke much too quickly, swiping at something sharp near his throat. He tried to roll over, but found that his body was pinned to the bed. Thinking that he had finally come to face his greatest fear, his eyes snapped open wide.

"I am a representative of Castle Elfwood," Laela began, dressed in one of the lord's most precious green garments and holding a very expensive jeweled stiletto to his throat. "Call off your men."

"We had no reason to believe that you were who you claimed," Penwarden said harshly. He had finally washed for the audience.

Jaeme was not interested in any excuses his vassal had to offer. He leveled a single question.

"Will you help us fight the dragon?"

The expression on Penwarden's sharp features told Cedric that the man was about to deliver an excuse of some type. Before it came, the knight stepped forward and offered, "I think it is best to assume that Lord Penwarden's men are in no condition to aid us against the dragon, my lord."

Dec was aghast at the old knight's intercession. Why would Cedric willingly offer any assistance to the person who had sent him out on his own to die at the claws of a fire-breathing serpent? But a look into Cedric's face revealed that the words were meant to benefit Jaeme, who was shortsightedly going to insist on Penwarden's cooperation. Dec realized that making demands on the cowardly lord at this time would only make relations more difficult in the future.

"Very well," Jaeme replied, angrily stepping down off Penwarden's throne. "We will leave it at that for now."

"There is one matter I would like to take up with you, my lord," Penwarden said quickly. "Cedric is a knight of my court. I would like him to return to me."

"As to that, sir, you will have to ask Sir Cedric for the answer. My offer of lodgings is, of course, still open," Jaeme added, addressing the knight.

Cedric had no intention of returning to Penwarden. He would remain with Jaeme and Elfwood for as long as he was allowed. Without glancing back, he strode from the Great Hall.

"And now, Lord Penwarden, there is a matter I would take up with you," Jaeme continued when the old knight had left the room. The young lord stepped forward, his manner so menacing that Penwarden shrank back. "I sent an envoy here not two days past. Where is he?"

Penwarden held his hands up in fear and denial. "I know not, my lord. We did send a man away who claimed to be from Elfwood. He could have been one of *them*!"

"In which direction did he ride?" Jaeme demanded furiously.

"Around the Wycham. But the dragon has made its home there, and only last night did I see a great gout of flame from that place. If your friend rode there—"

"If my friend rode there, Lord Penwarden, you will have much to answer for!"

His anger rising to a level he had never felt before, Jaeme turned on his heel and strode from the room, gesturing for everyone to accompany him. Sensing the depth of the young lord's ire, Dec, Laela, Desmond, and Sir Kipp were all silent as they followed him out.

Penwarden moved to sit back in his throne, brushing at the seat first with a look of distaste. He pulled out the dagger Laela had rudely awakened him with and dug its tip into his thumb, drawing a line of blood which he cleaned away with his tongue.

[illegible]

[illegible]

[illegible]

[illegible]

[illegible]

[illegible]

[illegible]

[illegible]

[illegible]

[illegible]

[illegible]

[illegible]

Chapter 15

THE PATH TO THE DRAGON WAS EASY TO FIND, BUT JAEME WAS NOT sure that he wanted to encounter the great serpent so quickly. He had hoped for some time to build up his courage and steel himself to face the monster again. He sighed heavily from atop Firebrand in disappointment.

"What is the matter, my lord?" Cedric asked from the young lord's right.

Jaeme gave the old knight what was intended to be his best look of lordly consternation, but he was sure it came off as something less noble and filled simply with fear.

"Ah," Cedric said, giving a sage nod. "There is no shame in it, my lord."

"Thank you for saying so, Sir Cedric," Jaeme replied leadenly. "I believe this is no way for a lord to act."

"Is that the lord's own truth? If I may speak candidly, what is the exact number of sovereign rulers you have known?"

Jaeme hesitated before answering, confused. "Only my father."

"Then in whatever manner you choose to conduct

yourself must be the best way, as you have but one example to model yourself upon,'' the knight said, turning back to face into the fog and rolling, hidden landscape.

The young lord took the noble's point to heart, though there was some remaining doubt. Jaeme guessed that the man had been attempting to bring some cheer in his own way, that of chivalry and honor. He remembered that his father had often said, ''From strength, build strength.'' To Jaeme, the old knight was certainly the strongest in many ways of all the nobles present.

The young lord looked behind him and caught occasional glimpses of Dec and Laela. He had ridden ahead of them both, still unforgiving of the mission the druidess had performed. The fact that she had not been hurt did not soften his feelings despite the great sense of relief. Dec, since his return, had done little but concentrate on his leather book of spells, studying it diligently to perfect every intonation and gesture. Every once in a while the mage would ask something of the druidess and Jaeme saw that her answers were short, almost curt.

''Cedric, there is much of knighthood that I would like to discuss with you,'' Jaeme began haltingly, unsure where his statement was leading, ''but there are also some questions about—other matters, for which I crave your advice.''

''You have but to ask of it, my lord,'' the old knight replied. He continued to gaze forward into the rampart of mist. He knew that the young man was going to ask questions better left to fathers, but the new lord had no father. Cedric decided to grit his teeth and bear whatever was to come.

Jaeme gathered his thoughts about him, still confused on why he had spoken. There was a swirling mass of events that caused questions to appear, then disappear just as quickly. He decided merely to open his mouth and give voice to the first thing that came to mind.

''How do I as lord deal with a woman who is my counselor?''

''How do you mean, my lord?''

Jaeme lowered his head and stared at Firebrand's rich

mane. Now that he had blurted his question, he was ashamed to have to pose it in better detail. However, he had brought himself to this point, and now, in the interests of good manners and good friendship, he would have to continue.

"There is a woman who I think I have certain—feelings for," he began lamely, hoping to be ambiguous and avoid any embarrassment, "yet she continues to confound me."

"I see," Cedric replied gravely with a frown. "I see there are two items you must address before your original question can be answered."

"And they are?"

"First you must decide if you have feelings, as you put them, or not," the old knight answered.

Jaeme saw where that would be important. "And secondly?"

Cedric let out a short laugh, one that seemed to be tinged with irony. "You must decide how she confounds you."

Jaeme nodded his understanding. "You are as wise as I knew you must be, Sir Cedric."

"No wiser than those that taught me, my lord. And they are many and several." After a few minutes of silence, Cedric added, "If it brings solace, let it suffice to say that my dealings with amour have been—educational."

Jaeme laughed loudly, making everyone in the company within earshot turn and look at him. He looked back at Laela and Dec and waved once, giving the druidess a wide smile.

"I was not sure if I would be able to be on the same footing with her, but now I see that I can," the young lord said to Cedric, who smiled tightly and kept his eyes on the road.

The druidess rode up on her horse, and for the sake of decorum, Jaeme fell back from his place near the old knight.

"What is so funny, my lord?" she asked with some hesitation.

"We are, Laela, and there is no need to call me 'lord' in private."

On inspiration, Jaeme leaned over and kissed the druidess lightly on the cheek. He stared into her eyes, and she felt the wall of ice she had created between them melt away, giving wing to her hope. She wanted to take him in her arms and hold him and be held in return, but on horseback she did not think this a prudent move.

"Jaeme," she began softly. "I am so sorry for making you give in to my plan. I thought—"

The young lord put a finger on the woman's perfect lips, silencing her apology. "There is no need for words. I under—"

"Halt the column!" Cedric called out with an upraised arm. His horse had already stopped moving.

Jaeme and Laela rode to the fore, the new lord peering into the fog and asking, "What do you see?"

In the distance, the grey, choking mists thinned and curled as if repelled by an unfelt wind. Jaeme waited for a few moments but saw nothing more that was out of the ordinary.

"What does this mean, Cedric?"

"I have seen this once before, my lord, in the presence of the—"

"Dragon!" Laela whispered, sniffing lightly in the air. "There is death nearby, and the smell of flame. . . ."

The young lord looked to his companion, who seemed almost in a trance. He waved his hand in front of her eyes, but received no response.

Jaeme snapped his fingers for Dec, who eventually heard the sound and peered up from his book. When he saw that the army had ceased moving, he realized that something important was happening. With a careful squeeze of his legs, he guided the horse forward.

Dec looked at Laela in confusion, snapping his own fingers to see if that would wake the druidess from her strange state. On impulse, he took out a piece of lodestone from under his cloak and dangled it from a piece of string above her head. He had seen one of his teachers do this to determine what was afflicting a sick woman.

The stone turned several times until it finally settled in one direction, pointing back toward the thinning fog and the dragon at its eye.

"What is it, Dec?" Jaeme implored. "What do you know?"

Dec shrugged and put his stone away. "I haven't a clue. Maybe that spell she got from the Druidic Council is making her live the life of a dragon," he offered, skeptical of his own words.

"Will she awake?"

Dec could do nothing but shrug again, though he desperately wished he could perform some spell that would help. He knew nothing of "naming" magics, and wasn't sure that the druidess would ever escape the thoughts that he guessed were trapping her mind.

Cedric was satisfied in a way that made him angry at himself, satisfied because magic was turning back upon its user; he pushed the feeling away. The woman who could have been his daughter was ailing and there was nothing he could do. He wished sorcery had never entered his life.

"Laela," the old knight said, his voice hard and commanding. "Laela! Wake up!"

The druidess remained staring into the fog.

"Your friends need you, Laela. It is your duty to grant aid!"

Within her thoughts, Laela felt her wings grow tired and her neck too heavy to lift.

"You are a representative of the Druidic Council and counselor to the new lord of Castle Elfwood! You *will* awake!"

Still heavier, too heavy to move . . .

Cedric's anger showed in his face, but Jaeme saw something else, something in the old knight's eyes that betrayed a certain tenderness the young lord had not seen before. His respect and fondness for the noble swelled again.

"You could have been my daughter, Laela, and for that you must return, for the memory of your mother who could have been my wife!"

Jaeme was aghast at the words, but before he could speak, Laela's entire body went limp and she almost toppled out of her saddle. Cedric was quick to catch her, and he held her in his arms, stroking her hair gently. The druidess's eyes came back to life, but she did not attempt to leave the noble's embrace.

"How could you have left her?" she asked, almost too softly for Jaeme to hear.

Cedric shook his head slowly. "She was a druid," he offered simply. Jaeme understood what the knight meant in view of the man's opinion of magic and magicians, even those whose purpose was the protection of the wild; because of his beliefs, Cedric was obliged to leave that which he loved. Jaeme knew that this was a quality to be admired, but he felt pity as well, because there was no room for change.

"I think we have a problem," Dec said leadenly, pointing forward.

Everyone turned and stared as the mists slowly parted, allowing them to see most of the forbidding serpent that lay ahead. Its head was cradled in its huge forearms and its thick tail encircled the entire length of its body. Jaeme's blood ran cold with the second sighting of the monster, and for a moment he was paralyzed with dread.

Cedric put Laela back on her horse and put his helmet on his head, smartly snapping down the visor. He pulled his lance from its holder and loosened the sword in its sheath.

"What did you do the first time you encountered the dragon?" Jaeme asked as he got hold of his senses.

"Charged with lance, of course," the old knight replied, shifting in his saddle. He made sure his feet were firmly in his stirrups. He would get only one charge, and the shock of impact might send him sprawling if he wasn't firmly horsed.

"It seems that Sir Kipp's plan of driving the beast from the woods won't be necessary," Dec mumbled superfluously.

Laela held her arms out and closed her eyes, furrowing her brow in concentration. There was little thought in her action, and the single word that issued from her mouth like a breath of flame sounded like nothing any of her friends had heard before.

The druidess felt a struggle within her, to be a dragon, dark, soaring, powerful and ancient and wise. Rampage with claws and lash with tail, breathing fire that was the glory of her kind . . .

"No," she whispered. "I am Laelestequenstrutia and I am a human, but . . ."

"But nothing!" Jaeme said. "You are Laela and you belong with us!"

Laela's eyes flew open and her mouth opened wide to bite with the fangs she felt were scorched clean from fiery breath, but in the next instant she remembered her place among the people in the world and returned her thoughts to her own.

"The dragon is Charmed," the druidess muttered, finally lowering her arms. In her eyes, which remained wide open, Dec thought he saw the iris change shape to that of a serpent's, vertical and thin.

"Excellent!" Jaeme blurted out happily. He turned from his friends and gazed out at the dragon, who apparently hadn't noticed the fact that it was under the influence of a powerful spell.

"What do we do with it now?" Cedric inquired flatly. He knew that *he* couldn't attack a foe unable to defend itself, even a foe as horrible as a dragon.

Jaeme put his head in his hands again, feeling the frustration mount with every passing moment. He heard the sound of approaching hooves and saw that Sir Kipp and Desmond had arrived at the front.

"What is the order, my lord?" Sir Kipp asked through his helmet. "Do we attack?"

"No, Sir Kipp. We do not."

"Yet there the beast lies!" the noble said incredulously. Like Cedric, he removed his lance from its holder.

Desmond nodded his agreement. "I do not understand."

"Let us finish it now, before it can cause more harm!" Sir Kipp added. His horse pawed uneasily at the ground.

"The beast cannot return the charge, good sir," Cedric muttered from within the confines of his helm.

"What?"

"It's the truth," Dec said, shrugging yet again. "Laela's put a charm on it, and now it will do whatever she says."

Despite the fact that the helmet covered Sir Kipp's features, Jaeme could tell that his chief commander was flabbergasted. The young lord remembered what one of the other nobles had said about this dragon being the chance of a lifetime to gain honor and glory. He could only imagine the immense disappointment that Sir Kipp must be feeling at being denied this singular opportunity, especially since the last battle to the serpent had been lost.

"Can't you make it just go away?" Dec asked Laela, who continued to stare at the monster.

"To where?" she shot back.

"I don't know. Back over the mountains or wherever it came from."

"That sounds like a reasonable plan," Jaeme added. His concern for Laela's welfare returned stronger than before as he realized that there might be some strain in maintaining the charm. "Can you do it quickly?"

Laela nodded once.

The dragon opened its eyes and gazed malevolently at the group gathered at the front of the army which was still hidden by the fog. Jaeme felt the power and age of its eyes on him again, as if he had been singled out among all the men in the land for revenge. He found that he was ready to shoulder that responsibility.

Within a moment, the dragon apparently lost its intense hatred and lifted its head slightly, seeming to listen for something as yet unheard. They all saw that the beast had continued to feed on the livestock of the surrounding pastures, leaving corpses everywhere in varying states of decay. For reasons that he did not quite understand, it was this image that Sir Cedric remembered most vividly.

The dragon continued to raise itself up, first its head, then its forearm. It lethargically pushed its body out of the cavity in the ground created by its immense bulk. The horses continued to paw at the ground uneasily, but the riders were heartened by the spectacle.

Something snapped in Laela's head. "Something's wrong," she intoned, losing the dreams of dragons and their glory.

The venomous light returned to the dragon's eyes, and it reared up on its hind legs with terrifying animation and roared its fury to the sky. Sir Kipp yelled an order to Desmond, who instantly rode back into the fog and bellowed the command anew. The low thunder of the army filled the plain.

Cedric lowered his lance and checked his stirrups one last time; Jaeme and Sir Kipp followed suit. Without waiting for orders, the old knight mumbled a prayer to his ancestors and began the trot that would lead to his last charge.

"Why do you attack?" the dragon demanded in a powerful voice that echoed throughout the land as its wings buffeted the air and sent dirt and loose scrub flying. "Why do you attack?"

"What?" Jaeme asked incredulously. Firebrand halted alongside Pele, halfway across the field.

"Why do you attack?"

The young lord was too stunned to reply. Of all the things in the world he'd thought he might see, a *talking* dragon was among the least likely.

Cedric lightly tapped Jaeme's thigh with his shield. "Answer it, my lord."

"We—we attack because you threaten the lives of our people!" Jaeme called out. Like his falling out with Laela, he was not sure where this conversation was going to lead.

The dragon shifted his body slightly and regarded Jaeme from a new position, eyes ablaze like the flames it breathed. "I harm no one."

"We have heard—"

"You have heard wrong, little lord. A simple enough matter. You may leave me now."

Cedric could not believe what he was witnessing. For the first time in his life, he felt himself become giddy. "The audacity! The utter outrage!" he cried. His voice eventually cracked into laughter, and for the life of him he could not stop.

The echo of his laughter drifted back to Dec and Laela, who glanced at each other in confusion. Dec looked back at the man who had been the model of a perfect knight and suddenly understood.

"Don't you see?" he said to the druidess, who stared at him blankly. "This is so *wrong*." The mage felt himself beginning to laugh as well.

Neither Sir Kipp nor Laela saw the humor in any of this. The knight wanted nothing more than to run the monster through with his lance or die in the attempt. The druidess felt somehow robbed of the opportunity to experience dragonhood more fully.

"All right, then! If you mean us no harm, what about this fog and the reports of evil?" Jaeme demanded, lifting his visor so that his voice might be more clear.

"As to that, the fog is an extension of the evil which sits even now upon your throne."

The dragon shifted to the right, moving its tail. Jaeme's eye was drawn to the motion and his heart nearly stopped when he saw what was revealed.

"Joseph!" the young lord cried out. Forgetting his place, he spurred Firebrand into motion. The dragon moved out of his way.

Jaeme jumped down off his mount before it had stopped moving. He fell to his knees and rose, only to stumble as he neared his friend. Jaeme looked into Joseph's face and saw death.

"What have you done?" he demanded of the dragon.

"I have done nothing. This man was set upon not long ago by the evil in the fog. I fought them off, but not in time."

The dragon's voice was like the roar of a conflagration and the crack of lightning across the sky, yet Jaeme heard almost nothing. Joseph was so near dying that he was afraid to leave his side.

"Jaeme, there is something I must tell you," Dec said from behind; Jaeme did not turn. The mage had finally built up the courage to ride up near the dragon after he was sure Laela would be all right. "I spoke with your father, his ghost, that is. He spoke of this evil and what it could mean to the rest of the world."

"Your friend speaks the truth, young lord. This fog is graver than you think," the dragon added. Dec felt that his statement carried a certain potency when confirmed by a dragon.

"What do you mean?" Jaeme asked, ignoring the fact that his father had spoken to another. Joseph's skin was very cold to his touch.

"I can't be sure because it seemed your father could not say what he desired," Dec began, slowly piecing together whatever he thought would be useful. "He said that you must protect the Elfwood forest because its magic was the life of the world."

With a final touch to Joseph's pale cheek, Jaeme stood and turned, his face grim. "I do not understand this evil. What can I do to fight it?"

The dragon lowered its head to the level of Jaeme's body. "That is something you shall find when you return to Elfwood," it said.

"The flame from the other night," Jaeme said slowly as he stared into the serpent's fiery eyes. "You were defending Joseph."

"True enough," the monster replied. Dec actually thought it was being humble as it dipped its head.

"Then I owe you a great debt," Jaeme answered, his voice loud and strong. "Name your reward."

Regaining its full height, the dragon peered out over the heads of the riders, swaying its neck slowly, as if searching for something. After a moment, it said, "This evil is more than you bargain for, little lord. You will require my assistance to vanquish it."

"Then, again I ask you to name your reward."

"I require little. Nothing more than twenty head of cattle a year and the freedom to go where I please. Do not worry," it hastened to add before Jaeme could object, "I, like a knight, will not abuse my privilege."

Cedric stayed his ground as the serpent's claw came dangerously close to his head, pointing to him as an example. He had the urge to swing at it with his sword, but the humor that had overtaken him continued to rule his heart.

"Your offer is fair, and I accept as Lord of Elfwood," Jaeme replied.

"And as to that, these lands are mine. I and mine own have lived in these hills since long before Offa's first stone was ever placed." The dragon dipped its head low again, this time menacingly. "As long as that is clear."

Jaeme, the new Lord of Elfwood, shook his head in negation. "That is not so, and to say it is implies disrespect for my station and that of my ancestors."

The serpent bowed its head again and muttered, "As for the memory of ancestors, those of my kind have much respect."

Jaeme bowed his head in respect as well, thinking of this great beast now as nothing more than another diplomat from a different country.

"But now for my part of the bargain. Those who attacked your friend are not of this life," the serpent began in a voice so clear that it made Dec remember to question how the beast could speak at all. "They prey on the—souls of others. They live and exist by certain rules to which they must adhere."

"And they are?"

"Asking permission to enter your home," Dec blurted out.

"For a magician, you are most astute," the dragon said. Dec was not so sure he wanted to take that statement as a compliment. "Your little sorcerer is correct. And you have given Katherine just that permission."

The name of the mysterious cloaked woman brought both Jaeme and Laela to their senses. They had each encountered Katherine under different circumstances. When Jaeme glanced at Laela, he realized his experience with her was not actually as comfortable as he had originally perceived. He remembered acting boisterous, disturbingly out of character.

Jaeme bolted into action, jumping back atop Firebrand. "Who will take care of Joseph?" he inquired of the great serpent.

"He will be safe here, and will return to life if the armies of evil are destroyed, as will all."

"Then sound the order to move! We must return to Elfwood!"

Chapter 16

EVERY HOME AND BUILDING IN THE VILLAGES THE ARMY PASSED through was boarded up. Many families had fled to the south; the others were too frightened to leave their homes. The ones who remained acted very much like the men at the walls of Castle Penwarden and offered nothing but hostility to any soldier who knocked upon their door.

The landscape was still covered under the swirling mists. Despite the fact that he wore a cloak as well as full armor, Jaeme shivered from the cold, which had become so fierce that icicles hung from roofs and tree branches. No man could tell if the time was night or day, or if the sun was indeed still alive in the heavens.

The journey to Elfwood was quicker than Dec had expected. He assumed that the influence of the dragon dissipated the chocking fog as it seemed to do upon the field and in the forest. Every once in a while the mage would glance back over his shoulder and he would think that the number of men diminished as the leagues rolled by.

When the contingent was halfway back, he was sure.

"Jaeme!" he whispered, afraid that even the slightest

sound would alert some unseen horror hiding in the hanging grey clouds. "The men—"

"I know, Dec. Stay close. I don't want to lose you as well," the young lord returned from the confines of his helmet. He hoped no fear crept into his voice.

By the time the army reached Elfwood, only a handful of men remained. None were able to explain what had happened to their comrades. All were deathly afraid.

Jaeme ordered a halt a hundred feet from the gate, which hung open on its hinges like the flesh from a gaping wound. The black caravan that had waited outside the walls of Elfwood for so long was gone, making the young lord think that whoever had been inside the wagons had finally been given leave by Katherine to depart and spread their malevolence across the land. He guessed that it must be they who caused such panic among the farmers.

With an expression so grim that he was glad none could see his face, Jaeme rode among their ranks with Desmond and Sir Kipp, two of the few nobles remaining.

"The dragon has told us that naught but courage will save our lives," he said in a low voice, riding among the men. He saw they looked up to him in a way that he had never expected: there *was* courage, and there was hope and respect. It heartened him greatly as he continued.

"If you believe in this evil, that there is something in the land that might end the world, then by the same token you must also believe in good. And in believing in good, you know that it is right, it is powerful, and it will always prevail."

Jaeme left his men with that thought. He had not heard the speech before, nor had he rehearsed it on the return trip from Wycham Wood. It came from his heart and was pure and true.

"A most excellent speech, my lord," Cedric said through his own visor. His admiration for the young man increased dramatically.

"I have not heard such inspirational phrases in quite some time," Sir Kipp added with a salute.

The new Lord Elfwood bowed to each of these compliments, but he did not stop Firebrand from continuing up the road. With a wave of his arm, he commanded the remaining soldiers of the army to follow.

Laela felt the cold creep back into her flesh again, as it had when the fog first appeared. Whatever evil chilled the mists seemed as draining as a cold stream; it made her body tremble. She found, however, that the chill left her bones if she concentrated on Jaeme's back as he rode on his proud charger into the darkness of his own home.

Dec could not remember ever having been so fearful. He thought his friends completely mad; they were riding into death's own gate without a second thought, and all Jaeme had to offer was philosophical claptrap.

The mage shook his head in confusion and took out his spellbook, going over the single cantrip he had prepared for this encounter. It was quite ambitious, but he felt that the danger involved to himself would be worth the effort considering that if the remaining army didn't succeed, the entire world was doomed.

Finally within a charge-move of the gate, Jaeme could see that little had changed physically in the keep. But there was something *spiritual* that had changed, becoming as twisted and as evil as he had imagined but refused to admit. Only the strength in his heart kept him pressing forward into his home which stood as silent as a gravestone to the memory of Elfwood.

Firebrand danced a few steps as his hooves crossed the threshold, making the young lord think that the ground was hot. The frost and fog, which had finally penetrated the gate because of an ignorant act on his part, showed this not to be true. Jaeme pressed forward, though his faithful mount continued to step unevenly.

''Welcome to your home, Lord of Elfwood,'' a thin voice said from within the fog. The words swam mockingly around Jaeme, but his courage did not falter. Laela and Dec heard the voice as well, and the magician moved his horse closer to her's for some small comfort.

''Show yourself, Katherine!'' Jaeme called out, his voice echoing against the inner walls of the castle as he remembered its doing when he was a child. "Show yourself so I may force you from my keep!"

"Strong words from such a young man," Katherine answered from nowhere. "Have you allies with you?"

Jaeme's right hand went to his father's sword; he felt that something was about to happen. "My only allies are my stalwart soldiers and the courage in their hearts."

"Then you have no allies," the woman replied.

The mists in the castle proper thinned, and within moments Jaeme could see the baleful eyes of soulless minions glaring from the shadows. He turned to hearten his men and saw that the gate had mysteriously closed, trapping everyone inside. There were less men now than had entered.

"Let us begin this fight before they gain the advantage," Cedric said at Jaeme's left side. The knight admired the aplomb with which the new lord approached his enemies; he thought it worthy of song.

For the first time, everyone heard Katherine's light laughter, which, to Jaeme's thinking, held an equal mix of confidence and sorrow.

"Tell us of yourself, woman!" the old knight commanded, riding to the fore. He looked up at the tower closest to the Elfwood and shouted, "By whose authority do you corrupt the lives of children?"

"I answer to none but mine own code, Sir Knight. As you answer to only your own," Katherine replied, her voice emanating from the tower where Cedric stared. "And in that, you know the price and the glory."

Beneath his visor, Cedric's face wore a troubled frown. He wondered if the fog could carry his voice across the distance to wherever Katherine had waited for this final moment. It was disconcerting to discover that this foe knew of the grief he'd suffered by adhering to his principles.

The old knight suddenly snapped his head up. "You'll not bring me down before the fight, devil!" he bellowed, shaking his fist in the air. "If you regret your life so, leave it!"

"As to that, I can only answer that such a feat would not be possible. With the taking of this keep and your deaths, the fate of the world is sealed by darkness. Now it is time for you to leave your life to me and offer your soul to the Abyss!''

Dec was the first to act. He began chanting his spell, the cantrip he had taken from the hidden scroll in the great library of the Magisterium Lundinium. It had first caught his eye because of the brilliantly colored illumination. He now saw that picture as the means of saving his friends' lives.

The wave of creatures that attacked was appalling both in number and appearance. Jaeme drew his silver blade and felt the hands of his father guiding his arm, cutting clean strokes through the bones and sinews that might have once belonged to the living. Greying flesh was rent with each attack, and Firebrand pawed at the air with a fury that matched that of the soulless masses.

Cedric found himself pressed back by a wave of silent hunters with eyes as cold as steel and hearts blacker than night. With this first charge he guessed that they must have been humans who had lost themselves to the evil of Katherine and whatever hell-sent monarch for which she was the herald. The lance became useless as the quarters of fighting were quickly closed. The old knight drew his sword, using his shield as a weapon to gain some time.

Like Cedric, Sir Kipp and Desmond quickly discarded their lances and fought side by side until Desmond's horse fell from under him, brought down by a sea of clawed hands that rent the animal's flesh until its blood spilled and steamed on the thirsty ground. Sir Kipp tried to help the trainer onto the back of his own horse, but Desmond elected to fight from where he stood, attacking with such fervor that over twenty of the grey minions were hewn before the next wave appeared. When it did, Sir Kipp used his steed to charge the oncoming monsters like a battering ram, jumping off the horse at the last moment to fight with Desmond, back to back.

Laela saw no end to the number of the dead that surrounded her. They never stopped, coming out of the fog and shadow of the castle walls to stagger forward on legs too thin to support their weight. Fangs protruded from their emaciated skulls. Laela's body changed to that of a bear and her claws matched theirs. Her hide was soaked with their lipid blood.

The soldiers formed a small square, using their spears as makeshift pikes to create a deadly phalanx. Dec stood in the middle of these men, continuing to chant his stolen spell, his presence giving the men-at-arms the confidence they needed to maintain their position despite the silent hordes that bore down upon them.

Dec remembered vividly the drawing, inked with bright reds and yellows and oranges. "The sun," he whispered to himself as he felt the flow of magic begin to churn within his soul. "Think of the sun."

Jaeme quickly realized that the only way to stay alive was to keep moving. Glancing quickly at Desmond and Kipp, who though sorely beset, were holding their own, he decided that Laela was the one who needed his assistance. Jabbing Firebrand in the side with his knee, the young lord slashed down twice into the face of an attacking creature, clawing its skull in two as the horse spun around and kicked backward, causing another temporary break in the attack.

Something hard struck Jaeme in the head; his ears rang and his sight dimmed. Without removing his feet from the stirrups, he leaned hard to one side and fiercely swung the magicked blade, bringing his body back up with the momentum before he could be unhorsed. The unholy creature who had jumped atop Firebrand lost its head down to the collarbone. Jaeme pushed the corpse off and pressed onward.

Laela had received several wounds that burned from scraping hands and biting fangs. She was beginning to tire and that made her panic. She understood that she did not have time to change into a hawk to escape, and she couldn't fight in the form of a bear for too long. Even if she could stand the fatigue, the spell would eventually wear off and she would become human again.

"Jaeme, help me!" she tried to cry, but the only sound that issued from her throat was a growl. Within seconds of her plea, she was nearly buried by a mass of attackers.

Cedric heard the bear's roar and knew that the druidess was in trouble. He sent Pele gracefully jumping into the air, crushing a dozen of the evil horde as the horse came to ground again and bolted for Laela. The sword in Cedric's hand was a halo of light as the blade swept in wide circles. He ignored the wounds to his legs and abdomen. They seemed to be on fire, and had not fully recovered from his injuries at the hands of the smith, but to save the woman who could have been his daughter, he would deny them all.

Dec fell to his knees and almost lost the thread of the spell. The heat from within his body made his skin blister on his fingers and ears, and he felt as if he might suddenly erupt in flames. He knew the spell required the Axiom of Sympathy, the like image of the sun creating the spell, but he had never known such a surge of power back into his body.

At the piercing cry of a dying soldier, Dec immediately fathomed the situation. The evil that created the fog and choked the sun must affect his magic as well. He now knew that Katherine must have some hold in the Elfwood, which meant that the world's magic was in danger of corruption. In the small section of his mind that was not concentrating on the spell, Dec realized that he must find a path back to the source of the pure magic or he would die.

Jaeme and Cedric converged at the same time on Laela and they proceeded to stab and stash at any of the soulless that came within sword reach. The young lord smelled his father's sweat, recognizing it from one of the few occasions when the two had practiced at swordplay together. He was glad for that time and would be glad for many more with his own son. It gave him strength to continue the fight.

Cedric's arm was a machine, a simple lever to cut and parry. Pele became a gristmill, and under its iron-shod hooves the minions were trampled into stillness. The old knight grew warm under his armor, a feeling he had not experienced since the wars against the Picts. He found himself recalling those times with a certain joy. The campaign had been successful, he had gained much honor and the praise of his sire. Now the battle was brought to the world and he could find nothing more noble than that.

The druidess was quickly extracted from her danger, and together the three friends moved toward the dark figures of Desmond and Sir Kipp. In a huge rush, Jaeme, Laela, and Cedric were beset by an incredible mass of attackers, and they offered themselves to the task with such abandon that the battle was over within minutes.

When they recovered their senses, they found that Desmond and Sir Kipp were nowhere to be seen.

The screams of the men-at-arms caused the horsemen to turn their mounts and wade back through the crowds of the soulless. Jaeme's armor was so battered that he had difficulty moving because the plates were scraping together, and Cedric had finally abandoned his helmet when three of his attackers had pounded on it with powerful fists. Laela had been wounded in the right arm and was bleeding badly; she knew that her form as a bear would last only a few more minutes; then, back in human form, she would succumb to shock. Even Pele had suffered an injury to his leg and was limping on occasion, though Firebrand had come to no harm.

Jaeme saw only a handful of his men remained standing, and even as his steed slowly plowed forward, walking up the ramparts of the dead, he saw three more soldiers die at the end of claw and fang. He also noticed that Dec was apparently uninjured, though the mage was kneeling on the ground as if in great pain.

"The sun! Find the sun!" the magician muttered to himself between clenched teeth. A small line of spittle formed a line from his mouth to the ground, but his mind was too far away for him to notice.

Only ten feet away, a wall of the soldiers' square collapsed, allowing the soulless to rush forward with madness in their cold eyes and not a word from their thin lips. The remaining men, still bolstered by Dec's presence, turned and tried to close the gap. Of ten, four were instantly killed and two more injured.

Jaeme and Cedric pushed their steeds forward so hard

that Pele's injured leg gave way, sending mount and rider to the ground. The bulk of the war horse smashed a great number of attackers, but the leg was broken and Pele could not stand. Cedric saw his mount's dilemma and leapt to his feet, swinging his blade one-handed and using his other hand to push the bodies away.

Firebrand filled the gap where the soldiers once stood, and the silver blade was like lightning in Jaeme's hand. Though the onrushing hordes were uncountable, he saw that he had dispatched a considerable number of them. Within moments he killed a dozen more, watching intently for Cedric's next move.

The old knight, kneeling at Pele's side, saw that the horse would never run again. It was a moment of great sorrow for him, though he suspected that not many others would know the meaning of losing a mount that had been a faithful companion through many glorious campaigns. When Cedric guessed he had brought himself enough time through his swordplay, he plunged the weapon into Pele's neck, killing him outright.

"Cedric!" Jaeme yelled as he and Laela finally reached the square. "We need you here!"

"For the last stand, my lord!" the old knight cried. Turning, Cedric bellowed with fury that he had finally been defeated. And by a woman! He quickly cut his way to the weakened square, feeling his back bleed and his legs throb from wounds.

"Then this is it, eh, my lord?" Cedric asked as he slashed two of the soulless at once, kicking their bodies away as their momentum carried the charge. "We are to lose the world?"

Jaeme tore his helmet from his head and used it to stop the charge of an attacker. "We yet live, Sir Cedric, and in that there is hope!"

Laela lashed out with her huge paws and growled as she crushed three attackers at once. She used their bodies to stop another rush, then fell back to the middle of the formation, where Dec had finally curled up into a ball.

"Laela! What are you—"

The druidess's form slowly shrank, brown fur fading gradually, becoming the red mane of hair that Jaeme had come to desire. Her right arm was bleeding badly, and the young lord could only watch as she fell unconscious to the ground.

Suddenly, the minions of evil stopped their attack, pulling back from the square of remaining men. Jaeme stared out into the courtyard that had once been home to so many happy memories but was now tainted with the bodies of stolen lives. The dead were an overwhelming tapestry of unmoving figures.

The soulless went on forever and Jaeme finally knew despair. Though his arm was not tired, neither he nor Cedric was capable of stopping them all. He finally understood the doom that lay in the fog.

"Let there be sun!"

Elfwood was covered in a blinding blaze of light. The strength that flowed through Dec into the spell made him feel he was standing in the middle of a raging river and he controlled its path. His blistering skin burned with such pain that a scream rose in his throat with each second the sun penetrated the fog and scoured the keep of its evil.

Jaeme shielded his eyes against the light and felt hope fill his heart. He had almost forgotten what it meant to bask in the light of purity.

Dec's scream grew beyond the range of his voice to create. His body was coiled tight and his bones shone in rough definition against his skin as his body strained against itself.

Cedric closed his eyes and tilted his face toward the fiery orb in the sky. Its heat brought back to him so many emotions that he could not begin to describe.

As suddenly as the light had began, it ended.

Jaeme found he could not see for several moments. When his sight returned, he discovered that the minions of evil were gone without leaving the slightest trace.

"What has happened, my lord?" Cedric inquired.

"I do not know, but I'm sure our mage friend can tell us."

Dec slowly rose to his feet. He held his shaking hands out, unsure what to do with himself. The pain he felt was so staggering that he was close to losing consciousness.

"The—the sun," he stuttered between cracked and bleeding lips. "I b-brought the s-sun."

"The sun must have destroyed them all," Jaeme suggested with a sweeping gesture of his sword.

Cedric shook his head and asked, "If that is the case, then why does the fog not lift?"

"Do you think this is victory?" the voice of Katherine inquired.

Stepping out from the shadows of the tower, Katherine showed herself to the men below. "These numbers meant nothing. I have a world to conquer!"

The dragon suddenly rose from the darkness outside the castle, its flame engulfing the woman, slamming her back against the wall with such force that the stones cracked where her body had struck. Without a word, the dragon released its fiery breath a second time.

Katherine lost her balance and fell over the castle wall to the ground below, but Jaeme thought he saw her arms flailing, trying to catch her balance. To him that meant she yet lived.

"Open the gates!" he cried, heedless of whatever horrors might await outside. "We must give help!"

There were only fifteen of the original number of soldiers left. Most of them were in shock, but they humbly followed Jaeme's command. As a single force, they attempted to push the door open, but it would not budge.

Black lightning cracked the air on the other side of the wall, and the dragon's head was wreathed in electricity as it released another bolt of fire. Its wings buffeted the air with such strength that even the dust within the castle proper was stirred into motion.

"Open it from the gate tower!" the young lord commanded, adding his strength to that of the men, using his back for better leverage. He wished he could help Laela, who lay unconscious on the ground, but he couldn't stop now. He had to get outside to save the world.

Cedric also joined those at the door, but then, deeming the effort futile, he abandoned his position and ran across the courtyard, picking up his shattered lance as he went.

"Cedric, where are you going?" Jaeme cried.

The old knight ignored the question and continued his charge, racing up the stairs that led to the ramparts, ducking his head in time to avoid spillover from the great serpent's breath.

Jaeme continued to strain with the other men against the door, which finally budged but not enough to allow passage. Looking up, he gaped in wonder as Cedric jumped off the castle wall, broken lance held point down. He heard the man's glorious cry to battle.

The sound of the unseen duel outside the walls drowned out the exertions of the men at the door. They were beyond exhausted and running on nothing but faith, but Jaeme could not allow them to cave in now.

"Push, you men!" he cried, feeling the gate open a fraction more. "Push! For all your worth, the world depends on us!"

With a last shove, the gate opened and all the men spilled out. They charged with screams of fury in their throats, leaping over the huge log that had been placed to block the gate. Jaeme charged with them, leading them to battle to save the Elfwood.

Katherine's body was impaled on Cedric's lance, into her chest, out her back, and into the earth. Jaeme saw that her pale flesh was beginning to decay and rot.

The old knight lay on his back, across the dragon's right claw, holding a hand over a wound that refused to be stanched. The dragon had a similar wound across its throat. Many of its scales were charred black, and more were rotted.

"You have your victory, little lord," the great serpent said in its cyclone voice.

Jaeme staggered forward, finally sheathing his silver blade. "But at what cost?" he said in anguish, going to Cedric's side.

The old knight smiled, genuinely and openly. "What matters the cost, my lord? The world is surely saved."

"True enough," the dragon added, bringing its head lower to face Jaeme and fix him with its burning red eyes. "Your battle has been fought and won."

"Was it not your battle as well?"

The dragon bobbed its head to the right, a gesture which the young lord took to be a shrug. "Perhaps. Eventually. Dragons live a long time."

"But not forever," Cedric said, rising painfully to his feet. His breathing came in ragged gasps, but he maintained his composure, clamping his other hand over the wound.

Dec shuffled around the corner, still holding his hands out from the pain. He did not know what was happening, but wanted to be of assistance.

"Here, Master Mage," Cedric called out, though it made him break out into a fit of coughing that brought blood to his lips. "Here. I have something for the one who saved our lives."

Dazed as he was, Dec sensed that something was wrong with Cedric, but he understood little else. He staggered onward only because he was called, not because he understood the gravity of the situation.

The old knight reached under his armor and pulled out his signet ring. He held it in his hand, feeling its weight in his palm. "I want you to have this, Decutonius Consulus. It is the last symbol of my family's honor. I give you the honor you so dearly sought."

Cedric tucked the ring into the magicians belt, and for the first time did not feel regret that he would be the last of his line. Dec blinked his eyes rapidly, tears flowing though he could not understand why.

The knight turned to face Jaeme, who also had tears in his eyes. Cedric stood before the new Lord of Eldwood and tried to gauge how this young man would rule his domain. He saw only hope, and perhaps a little happiness.

"Will you accept service at Castle Elfwood, Sir Cedric?" Jaeme asked through gritted teeth.

Cedric shook his head slowly, closing his eyes for a

moment against the pain that threatened his life. "No, my lord, I cannot. Do not begin your reign with death."

Jaeme stepped back and nodded, offering the same comradely gesture that Sir Kipp had offered Desmond so long ago. Smiling, the old knight returned the salute.

"It is time to go, Sir Knight," the dragon said, lowering its body gently to the ground. "The halls of my ancestors await."

"As do the spirits of mine," Cedric replied. The knight turned and walked back toward the dragon, but he fell on one knee and dipped his head, beginning to fall over. Before Jaeme could offer his aid, Cedric stood again, hand still clasped to his side.

The knight climbed upon the dragon's shoulders and the serpent raised its neck so its rider would not fall off. The beast made a last survey of the castle and surrounding country and slowly beat its wings, creating a blinding storm of dust.

A moment later it stopped, bending its neck low again so Cedric might speak the final words that were on his mind.

"Jaeme!" he cried out over the settling winds. "If you truly love her, she will confound you."

The new Lord of Elfwood smiled and nodded his head in understanding.

And then his friend was gone.

Chapter 17

DEC CRANED HIS NECK AND FELT THE BONES CRACK. THOUGH HIS hands were still in bandages and Laela had applied more of the rancid poultice to his flesh, he continued to write in his journal.

And that is the tale, he penned, attempting to think of a way to finish the entry he had been working on for the better part of the week. *I have returned to Castle Elfwood as the resident magician and Jaeme has returned to his throne.*

Jaeme's face does not hold the mirth it had when I first arrived, and this I can fully understand. He has seen the ghost of his father and the death of friends, and there is no man who is not changed by the fight for his life, his hearth, and his home. So much has happened in the past weeks that there are barely words to describe how the young lord must be feeling. He has seen to the harvest for the winter and has sent word to Albion of the events that transpired here, and in that he has been efficient, though his appearance is haggard. Laela seems the only one who gives him respite.

Laela herself had again gone to her home in the forest amongst the druids to see her foster mother and also to assist with the restoration of the Elfwood. Her arm is scarred by the wounds from the battle in the castle proper and she strokes it without noticing when she stares out into the darkness. Other than that, she is cheerful and has good reason. What could be worse than the events which have recently transpired?

The people in the villages have returned to their homes and fields. They are all prepared for the winter, fortunately having lost only a few weeks worth of their crops to the cursed fog that once choked the land. Many did not return, and I venture to say that many more were lost to Katherine's hellish scheme. But like Laela, they still smile when their children play.

I was contacted by the Magisterium Lundinium. It seems that Albion, and all other lands, were also engulfed by the mysterious fog. And like Castle Elfwood, the keep of our king received silent visitors in black wagons. But unlike at Elfwood, few suffered on the island and the cold had been their only adversary.

According to the Magisterium, the hold that Katherine had on the world for a short moment was enough to block all attempts at communication, and no aid could be sent through magical means. It was equally impossible to set ships to sail, as they became lost the moment they weighed anchor. A few of the older magicians on Albion died in the attempt to gain insight into the fog and its creation; among them was one of my professors, Andelaine. He was the one that always warned me I would come to nothing if I didn't change my childish ways. He will be missed by all.

My parents are well, and did not suffer during the past few weeks. I would like to visit them now for some much needed rest, but Jaeme might need my assistance and so I must stay.

Together, Laela and Jaeme seem truly happy. I admit that for quite some time I hoped that she might be more attracted to me than to him, but I see now that they belong together. Jaeme has made memoriams for both Sir Kipp and Desmond, hanging the shirt of punishment in the main hall next to his father's silver sword.

For myself, I have dreams of that night when I called the sun down to cleanse the world, but can only see Cedric through the haze of the tears that wake me. I have the knight's signet ring, and it is heavy and I will bear it forever in his name and memory. I wonder if it is as heavy as the burdens which he placed upon himself, as heavy as the love he once held for a druidess's mother. I wonder if he has finally found the honor he forever sought in a world where his number have faded and been replaced by the petty schemes of thieves. I wonder if he ever knew how deeply he tempered my life.

I hope he has.